HANGROPE LAW
A Rancho Diablo Story
by Colby Jackson

Colby Jackson

The Rancho Diablo Series

Shooter's Cross
Hangrope Law
Dead Man's Revenge

Copyright © 2010 by James Reasoner

Ebook Version Published January 2011
CreateSpace Version Published July 2011
The Book Place, P.O. Box 931, Azle, TX
76098 bookplc@flash.net

1

Titus Blaylock eyed the trees warily as he rode toward them. He knew the Comanches were in there, just waiting to charge out, chase him down, shoot him off his horse, and scalp him.

Of course, he only had to worry about the Comanches if those outlaws hidden in those rocks to his left didn't ambush him. Which they probably would. A dozen of the meanest, bloodthirstiest owlhoots in the whole state of Texas were waiting for him, intent on shooting him full of holes.

They were in for a big surprise when he whipped out the pair of revolvers holstered on his hips and started blazing away at them. Left, right, left, right, one gun after the other roaring and spitting hot leaden death at the varmints . . . Wipe 'em all out, that's what he'd do, and when he was finished killing outlaws, why, he'd charge right into the thick of those painted savages and make them sorry they'd ever gone on the warpath. Yes, sir, by the time the famous gunslinger Titus Blaylock was through with them, those outlaws and Comanches would be sorry they had ever dared to venture onto

Rancho Diablo.

"Yeee-hah!" With all the sheer exuberance of his sixteen years, Titus let out a whoop as he leaned forward in the saddle, dug his boot heels into the horse's flanks, and sent the animal racing alongside the Brazos River.

One of these days, he thought. One of these days, all the adventures he dreamed about would come true.

In the meantime, he could live out those adventures in his head and enjoy the feel of the wind in his face as he galloped over the rugged landscape of his father's ranch.

What made it even better and more satisfying was that Elijah and Miriam were back home, tending to his chores for him. Let them get the weeds out of Ma's garden this week. Elijah didn't mind the work; he was the sort who would rather read about somebody having adventures in a book than get out and have some of his own, and Miriam, well, Miriam was just a girl, no matter how much she might wish she had been born a boy so she could get out and raise hell like her brothers. One of her brothers, anyway.

Who could stand around on a beautiful spring day like this and get blistered hands from chopping weeds with a hoe, anyway? The trees were blossoming, the wildflowers were blooming, the wind was warm and sweet, and the Texas sky was the deepest, clearest blue Titus had ever seen. It was a day for adventuring, not working.

Titus reined the horse back to a walk. He intended to be gone from the ranch house all day, and he didn't want to wear out his mount too quickly. He paused to watch the Brazos River make its slow, stately way past him.

He had looked at maps – that was one of the few things books were good for, sometimes they had maps in them – and had traced the course of the Brazos far, far up into the wilds of northwest Texas, where the Comanches still ran free. Someday he would follow the river all the way to its source, he vowed. That would be an adventure to tell stories about for a long time.

With a smile, Titus heeled his horse into motion again. He had passed the rocks where the imaginary outlaws were hidden, ridden through the trees where the Comanches of his own creation had been waiting to lift his hair. But there was a clump of brush ahead, next to the trail that followed the river, and what dangers might be lurking in it? Maybe a bear or a mountain lion, Titus thought. He could just see himself wrestling for his life with a bear or a big cat, using a Bowie knife to slay the beast . . .

Something moved in the brush.

Titus stiffened in the saddle and brought his horse to an abrupt halt as he stared at the branches swaying back and forth. Were there *really* bears or mountain lions in this part of Texas? His family hadn't lived here long enough for him to be sure.

But something was in there, and it let out a menacing growl.

Well, not really a growl so much as a moan, Titus thought after a moment, and when the sound came again, he could tell that it wasn't all that menacing, either. In fact, it was more like a noise somebody would make when they were in pain. He couldn't be sure about that, though.

The smart thing to do, he told himself, was to turn the horse around and light a shuck out of here, just as fast as he could, before whatever it was charged out of there in a killing frenzy.

He was about to do that when the thing in the brush said, "Help . . . help me . . . please . . . I can hear your horse . . ."

So it wasn't a bear or a mountain lion, but rather a man. A hurt man – or at least a man pretending to be hurt.

Titus swallowed hard, got a good grip on the reins and his nerves, and said, "Come out of there where I can see you, mister."

"I . . . I can't." The voice was thin and reedy, like it belonged to an old man. "You gotta . . . come in here and help me . . ."

It's a trap, a voice in the back of Titus's head warned him. *You go in there, you'll never come out.*

"I'll go find somebody – " he started to say.

"If you do, it'll be . . . too late. You got any . . . water?"

Involuntarily, Titus glanced down at the canteen hung on his saddle, right next to the sheath that held his Henry rifle. Both items helped him make up his mind.

"All right, mister," he said. "Hang on just a minute."

A weak chuckle came from the brush. "I ain't goin' anywhere . . . unless it's the fiery pit . . ."

Titus had heard enough preaching in his life to know what the man meant by that. He swung down from the saddle and drew the Henry from its sheath. Then he took the canteen loose and draped it over his shoulder by its strap.

"I've got a rifle" he said as he approached the brush. "If you're trying to trick me, I'll shoot you, sure as the sun came up this morning."

"No tricks," the unseen man told him. "Thank you, son, thank you . . ."

His voice trailed off and he didn't say anything else.

"Mister? Mister, you still there?"

That was a stupid question, Titus told himself. If the man really was hurt bad, he couldn't get up and run off, and if he wasn't hurt, he'd be lurking in there, waiting for Titus to get close enough to grab him.

Using the Henry's barrel to push the branches aside, Titus worked his way into the thick growth. He spotted the shape lying motionless on the ground ahead of him. The man's clothes were ragged and torn and covered with trail dust. A battered old hat lay upside-down on the ground near him, as if it had fallen off when he collapsed. Strands of thinning gray hair were plastered by sweat to his pale scalp. A gun butt with walnut grips stuck up from a holster on the man's right hip.

Titus had to swallow hard again. A part of him wished he was back home, fighting those dang weeds in the garden. He was scared, no doubt about that.

But at the same time, finding a wounded man like this was an adventure, wasn't it? And hadn't he been wanting to have an adventure?

The stranger was still breathing. Titus heard the rasp of air in the man's throat and said, "Mister, can you hear me? Mister?"

No response came from the man. Titus took a deep breath. He had to know what he was dealing with here. He approached the man with care and knelt beside him, setting the rifle aside so both hands were free. But he kept the weapon close, where he could get it in a hurry if he needed it.

He reached out and took hold of the man's arm. With a grunt of effort, Titus rolled him onto his back. For a second Titus was frozen by the sight of the weathered, leathery-skinned face and the ugly bloodstain on the man's shirt.

Then suddenly the man's eyes popped open and his claw-like hand shot out to clamp down with painful force on Titus's arm.

2

"He said *what*?" Miriam Blaylock demanded of her younger brother.

"That if we would take care of the garden for him today, he'd do our chores for the next week," Elijah Blaylock explained.

Miriam stared at Elijah for a long moment, wondering how anybody could know so much and still be so dang stupid. Elijah read books all the time, and in many ways he was canny beyond his thirteen years, but when it came to his brother Titus, Elijah always wanted to believe the best.

Miriam knew better. At fifteen, she was only a year younger than Titus and had had plenty of time to become familiar with his tricks.

"He was lying to you, you dolt," she said. "It's a pretty day and Titus didn't feel like working, so he made you a promise he never intends to keep. Tomorrow he'll have some excuse why he can't do his own chores, let alone take over ours even for a day."

Elijah thought about it for a moment and nodded. "You may be right."

Miriam bit back an angry response. It didn't do any good to get impatient and irritated with Elijah. Instead she asked, "Do you know where he was going?"

Elijah shook his head. "I don't have any idea."

They were standing in front of the shed built onto the side of the barn, where hoes, shovels, and pitchforks were kept. Elijah already had a hoe in his hand. He had been on his way to the garden – to do Titus's work! – when Miriam intercepted him.

Now she jerked a thumb over her shoulder toward the garden. All three of the youngsters had helped their mother Jenny plant it several weeks earlier, much to the dismay of Miriam and Titus. They had barely started exploring Rancho Diablo, the ranch that their father Sam had established a short distance upriver from the settlement of Shooter's Cross, Texas. To the northwest, the wooded heights of York's Peak dominated the view. The Brazos wound its way past the peak that had become famous during the Texans' war for independence from Mexico because of the exploits of one "Shooter" York, who had positioned himself on it to kill dozens of Mexican soldiers with well-placed rifle balls.

"If you want to hoe weeds in Titus's place, you go right ahead," Miriam said. "I'm going to find him and make him come back to do his own chores."

"Are you sure you're not just looking for an excuse to ride around the ranch?" Elijah asked.

"You hush," Miriam snapped. Why was her brother was so blasted smart when he wanted to be?

She went into the barn and found Gabby Darbins mending harness. The old, whiskery ranch hand looked up from his task and nodded a greeting to the redheaded girl.

"Howdy, Miss Miriam," he said. "Somethin' I can do for you?"

"Have you seen Titus today?"

Gabby scratched at his tobacco-stained white beard. "Matter of fact, I have. Seen him saddle up that hoss of his and ride off 'bout half an hour ago, I'd say."

"Which direction?"

"Believe he was headed north along the river."

That didn't surprise Miriam. She knew Titus liked the river and wanted to explore farther up the Brazos.

"Thanks, Gabby." She went to the stall where the paint pony she usually rode was kept.

"Are you ridin' out, too?"

"Just for a little while." Miriam gave the old-timer a dazzling smile. "You won't tell Pa, will you?"

A pained look came over Gabby's face. He was loyal to his boss, Sam Blaylock, but at the same time it was hard to say no to a beautiful young woman. With Miriam's trim shape and wild mane of red hair, she was definitely beautiful – and she knew it.

Gabby sighed. "All right. Just don't be gone long, hear? You want me to saddle that pony for you?"

"Hell, no," Miriam shot back with the boldness that had scandalized her elders on numerous occasions. "I can saddle my own horse."

She proved that by slapping the rig on the paint and leading the pony out the back door of the barn a few minutes later. She was blocked from view of the house here. She knew her father and mother were both inside. Her father was going over the books, trying to see how much money he was making from the sawmill he had built with the help of Gabby, Mike Tucker, Duane Beatty, and the big, tow-headed young man called Randy, who had started out trying halfheartedly to bushwhack Sam Blaylock and wound up working for him instead. Miriam's mother Jenny was in the kitchen seeing to the midday meal for the men.

Miriam insisted on wearing trousers most of the time, something else that scandalized folks along with her occasionally salty language. That made it easy for her to put a foot in the stirrup and swing up into the saddle. She pointed the paint away from the barn and clucked at it as she heeled it into motion.

She swung wide around the sawmill and headed for the Brazos, intending to pick up the trail upriver. She didn't know how far she would have to ride to find Titus, but he didn't have that much of a lead Even though he was older, she would make him regret trying to play such a mean trick on Elijah. She'd twist his ear half off if she had to, but one way or another she would bring him back to apologize and take care of his own chores.

She wished briefly that she had thought to bring along the old single-shot rifle her father had taught her to shoot. Her mother hadn't been too happy about that, but Sam Blaylock believed that all of his children should know how to handle a gun, even though at the same time he hoped they would never have to use one to protect themselves.

Miriam put that thought out of her mind. She wasn't going to run into any trouble. Rancho Diablo was her home. She ought to be safe here.

Part of the time the trail followed the course of the Brazos and ran close beside the river. In other places, hills and bluffs crowded right up to the bank, and the trail curved away from the water to avoid the rougher terrain. Miriam kept an eye out for her brother as she rode. Titus was a daydreamer, and it wouldn't surprise her if he had stopped and stretched out on some grassy hillside to stare up at the sky and indulge in some of his lurid, bloodthirsty fantasies.

She didn't see any sign of him, though, except some hoofprints left in the dusty trail by his horse. At least, she assumed those tracks had been left by Titus's mount. There shouldn't be anybody else roaming around up here. Rancho Diablo wasn't really a working ranch yet; the wild longhorns Sam Blaylock would use to build his herd were still scattered all over the range. So there weren't many ranch hands and no real stock-tending to take care of just yet.

Miriam frowned and a little shiver went through her as she thought about what might happen if she ran into any strangers up here, several miles from the house. She had never been the type to shy away from trouble, but she liked to think that she had at least a little common sense. Western men, even the worst of them, tended to be chivalrous where females were concerned, but a young woman out riding by herself like this might be a tempting target for a little sport.

"Blast it, Titus," she said aloud. "Why can't you stay home and do your own dang chores? And where the hell are you?"

There was no answer, of course, except the shrill cry of a bluejay as it took off from a tree ahead of her. Miriam guessed she had spooked it.

Or somebody else had.

Two men on horseback came out of the trees to her left, not quite galloping their mounts but still riding pretty fast. Miriam gasped in surprise when she spotted them. She hauled back on the reins and started to turn her pony, thinking that she would head for home as quickly as she could. Before she could move, though, one of the men shouted, "Hold it, girl!"

The paint was fast, but Miriam knew the men on those big, rangy horses could outrun her pony and catch her. If they had to chase her down, the effort might anger them, which could just make things worse for her.

Instead of fleeing, she sat on her horse and lifted her chin at a defiant tilt as she waited for them to reach her. She glanced toward a knoll on the other side of the pasture she had been crossing. Had something moved up there just now?

Miriam didn't know and couldn't worry about that. The two men were close enough now for her to see their cruel-looking, hardbitten faces, and the sense that she was in trouble was very strong in her. It was too late to run, too late to do anything but wait and see what these men had in mind for her.

3

Titus gasped and tried to pull away as the wounded stranger clutched his arm, but the man's grip was strong despite his injury. Instead of trying to hurt Titus, though, the man just licked his lips and croaked, "Water . . ."

"S-sure," Titus managed to say. "I've got it right here. If you'll just . . . let go of me . . ."

The man's bony fingers slid off Titus's arm. A grin pulled at his dry, cracked lips. "I didn't mean to . . . scare you, son . . ."

"I'm not scared," Titus said, his voice stronger now. He took the canteen off his shoulder and pulled the cork. Carefully, he put one hand behind the man's head and lifted it while he used the other to tilt the canteen to the stranger's mouth.

The wounded man drank like water hadn't passed his lips in a month. Titus let him gulp at the canteen for a few seconds, then pulled it away. The man looked like he wanted to protest but didn't have the strength. His head sagged back against Titus's hand.

"I'm . . . much obliged," he said. "I lost a mite of blood. That makes a man . . . thirsty."

"Are you shot?" Titus asked.

"Yeah. Took a bullet through . . . through my side. Got a nick on my leg, too. But I'll be all right, if you can . . . if you can help me get where I'm goin'."

"Where's that?"

The stranger grimaced as a fresh wave of pain seemed to go through him. After a moment it must have eased. He went on, "I'm lookin' for a ranch that's supposed to be somewhere in these parts. Fella who owns it is . . . an old friend of mine . . . name of Sam . . . Sam Blaylock."

Titus stared at the man in amazement. He was sure he had never seen this stranger before, so the man wasn't an old family friend, no matter what he said. But it was possible that he knew Titus's pa from a long time back. Sam Blaylock had grown up in the mountains of Arkansas, and Titus didn't know everybody who had ever been acquinted with him.

"Listen, mister," he said. "Sam Blaylock is my pa, and you're on his ranch, Rancho Diablo. If you can get up, you can ride my horse and I'll take you to him. Mister? Mister?"

It was no use. The wounded man had lost consciousness again.

Titus knelt there, at a loss what to do next. Choices raced through his head. He could leave the man where he was, mount up, and ride back to the ranch headquarters as fast as he could to fetch help. If he did that, though, it might be too late by the time anybody got back out here.

He decided that the best thing to do would be to get the man on his horse and ride double. That was the fastest way to get help. Both of Titus's parents had experience at patching up bullet wounds, and so did Tucker and Duane. They could at least stop the bleeding while somebody fetched a real doc from Shooter's Cross.

Titus was a tall, rangy young man, and even though he didn't particularly like to work, he had done enough of it in his life to make him pretty strong for his age. He slung the canteen over his shoulder again, got hold of the man under the arms, and lifted him. The man's feet and legs dragged on the ground as Titus hauled him out of the brush toward the horse. Titus had left the animal ground-hitched. The smell of blood must have spooked it, because it moved back skittishly. Titus lowered the man to the ground and grabbed the dangling reins. He tied them quickly to a bush and went back to get his rifle.

When he had the Henry in its saddle sheath, he knelt beside the man and said, "Mister? Mister, it'd sure be easier to do this if you'd wake up a little."

That didn't draw any response. Titus sighed, got behind the man, and took hold of him under the arms again. With a grunt of effort, he lifted the man and got him precariously balanced on his feet.

The stranger muttered, "Wha . . . wha' are you . . ."

"Good," Titus said. "You're awake. I didn't know how I was gonna get you in the saddle. Put your foot in the stirrup. I'll hang on to you so you won't fall."

Getting the semi-conscious man mounted was awkward and difficult, but finally Titus was able to boost him into the saddle. The man was aware enough of what was going on to wrap both hands around the horn and hang on. Titus jerked the reins loose and climbed up behind him. He had ridden double with Elijah enough times to know what to do. He turned the horse toward home and got it moving.

The stranger's head hung forward, and he swayed back and forth. He would have toppled out of the saddle if not for Titus's strong arms around him. A queasy feeling went through Titus as he realized the warm wetness soaking into his sleeve was the man's blood. In all his imagined adventures, he had never gotten blood on him.

The trail wound up a hill topped with live oaks. As Titus reached the crest, he saw something in the field down below. Three riders were sitting there, two of them flanking the third as if trying to hem that one in.

With a shock of recognition, Titus realized that the third rider was his sister Miriam. Nobody else around here rode a paint pony and had a bunch of flaming red hair. What was Miriam doing down there with two men who were also strangers, like the one sitting in front of Titus now?

Like all little sisters, Miriam was annoying as all get-out most of the time . . . but she was his sister, and Titus felt a fierce upsurge of protectiveness as he thought she might be in danger. His first impulse was to charge down that hill, confront the two men, and tell them to leave Miriam alone.

But he wasn't sure he could hold the wounded man in the saddle if he did that, and besides, he wanted to know what was going on. Holding his breath, Titus listened intently and tried to hear what was being said between his sister and the strangers.

Titus heard the words "old man" and "wounded" and something that sounded like "pike", although he couldn't be sure about that one. Then one of the men asked in a loud, distinct, and somewhat angry voice, "Have you seen him?"

They were looking for the man he had on the saddle in front of him, Titus realized.

Which meant they were probably the ones who had shot him.

The wounded man stirred. "Wha' . . .?" he said again. "Wh-where are we?"

"Shhh," Titus said. Those other strangers were armed with pistols and rifles, and their beard-stubbled faces looked plenty mean. He had to do something to help Miriam, but he wasn't sure what.

The gunslinger Titus Blaylock, the hero of all his daydreams, would have known what to do. That Titus Blaylock could have saved the day with no trouble at all.

Suddenly, though, *this* Titus Blaylock was about as far away from that one as you could get. His pulse pounded like a drumbeat in his head, and he couldn't seem to get his breath.

Down below, Miriam shook her head. " . . . don't know what you're talking about," Titus heard her say. She sounded scared, although she was trying to be bold as usual, and that made Titus even more upset. Her defiance might aggravate the men and get her into even worse trouble.

"Don't lie to us, girl," the other man said.

"I'm not lying!" Miriam insisted. "I haven't seen anybody like that." She started to turn her horse. "You'd better leave me alone!"

The strangers nudged their mounts to get in her way and stop her from fleeing.

The wounded man muttered, "You got a rifle . . . Help me get down."

"What?" Titus said.

"Get me . . . off this horse!"

The urgency in the man's voice made Titus move. He slid off the horse's back and reached up to help the man dismount. The man half-fell out of the saddle, but Titus grabbed him and kept him from collapsing. The man fumbled at the butt of the Henry and tried to draw the rifle out of its sheath.

"What are you doing?" Titus asked. "You can't – "

"You don't know those hombres," the old man replied. With a visible effort, he forced himself to stand straight and steady. "Gimme that rifle. That girl's in danger."

To Titus's dismay, he saw that the man was right. One of the strangers was reaching for Miriam now, and Titus heard his angry shout. "By God, we'll make you talk!"

Titus jerked the rifle out of its sheath. He would have used it himself, but the old man grabbed it and pulled it out of his hands before Titus knew what was going on. With swift, practiced ease, the man worked the Henry's lever, lifted the rifle to his shoulder, lined the sights, and fired.

4

It was a hell of a shot. Titus didn't even have time to worry that the bullet would hit Miriam instead of its intended target. At this range, that was a possibility, especially considering the shaky condition of the man who had fired it.

But the slug flew straight and true, and the man who was about to grab Miriam rocked back in his saddle before his hand could close around her arm. His horse started bucking. The man toppled off and fell limply to the ground, where he lay for a second with one foot hung in a stirrup. Then the horse bolted and dragged him across the field.

Titus had to give Miriam credit for thinking fast. She took advantage of the distraction provided by the shot to whirl her horse away from the other man and light a shuck for the trees on the far side of the open ground. The second man hesitated as if he were unsure whether to go after her or come after whoever had shot his partner.

He made up his mind and sent his horse charging up the hill toward Titus and the wounded stranger. A revolver appeared in his hand and spouted fire as the dull boom of a shot rolled across the Texas landscape. A second shot quickly followed the first one, and even though the range was long for a handgun, the bullet thudded into a tree trunk close by.

"Shoot him!" Titus called to the old man. "Shoot him!"

But when Titus glanced over at the wounded man, he saw to his horror that the man was passing out again. The rifle slipped from his fingers and fell to the ground. The man dropped to his knees and pitched forward on his face, either dead or out cold.

That left Titus with an angry gunman galloping straight at him and blazing away. He heard another slug whine through the branches overhead.

A few more feet and the man would be close enough for better accuracy, and Titus had no doubt the man would kill both him and his wounded companion, and Miriam, too. After all, those hombres had already tried to kill the old man once today.

Faced with no choice, Titus bent over and snatched the Henry from the ground. He levered a shell into the chamber and raised the rifle to his shoulder. It seemed to weigh a ton and he was so scared that his heart felt like it was going to burst out of his chest, but he settled the sights on the rider as best he could and squeezed the trigger.

The Henry had quite a kick to it. The recoil sent Titus staggering back a step. As he caught his balance, he saw the man clutch his shoulder and sway violently in the saddle. *I hit him!* Titus thought. *I actually hit him!*

But would it be enough to make the man break off his attack? In case it wasn't, Titus set himself and worked the Henry's lever again. By the time he had the rifle ready to fire, the rider had veered off his course. He was turning in a wide loop, riding hunched over now like he was in pain, which he had to be, considering that Titus had ventilated his shoulder.

The man galloped off to the west, disappearing over a ridge. Titus watched him until he was gone. It was possible the man would try to double back, but Titus didn't think it was very likely, wounded like he was.

He caught a flash of red hair from the corner of his eye and looked across the field to see that Miriam had returned. Her curiosity must have gotten the better of her. She sat on her horse at the edge of the trees and peered across the open ground. Titus stepped out where she could see him, waved an arm over his head, and shouted, "Miriam! Miriam, over here! It's me!"

She rode toward him, taking a course that would allow her to skirt widely around the body of the man the old-timer had shot out of the saddle. The man's foot had come loose from the stirrup after his horse had dragged him for a hundred yards or so.

While Miriam was doing that, Titus hurried over to the old man and knelt beside him, just as he had in that thicket of brush earlier in the morning. He took hold of the man's shoulders and rolled him over onto his back. Relief went through Titus when he saw the man's chest rising and falling. He was still alive and had just passed out again.

But as much blood as he had lost, that couldn't keep happening. One of these times, the old man would lose consciousness and not come to again. Titus felt even more urgency now to get this stranger back to the ranch house.

"Titus! Titus, where are you?"

"Over here!" he returned his sister's shout.

Miriam rode up a moment later. She was fair-skinned to start with, and the events of the past few minutes had left her even paler. When she saw the wounded old-timer, she said, "Oh! Who's that?"

"I don't know his name," Titus replied, "but I reckon he may have saved your life when he shot that fella. Help me get him back on my horse."

Miriam dismounted and lent her strength to Titus's. Together they were able to lift the old man onto Titus's horse. If he hadn't been built sort of spindly-like, they probably wouldn't have been able to do it. Once they had him in the saddle, Titus climbed on behind him again and told Miriam, "Put my rifle back in the sheath."

As she did so, she asked, "Did you shoot that man, Titus?"

"This fella shot the first one, the one that's still laying down there, but I had to shoot the other one."

The matter-of-fact way he was able to say it surprised even him a little. He hadn't had any choice in the matter. It had been a life-and-death situation, and he'd done what he had to do.

He couldn't help but be a little proud of himself, too.

Miriam swung back up onto her pony and they started down the hill, moving slowly so Titus could hang on to the old man and keep him on the horse. As they rode, Titus kept an eye on the man lying in the field. After being shot and then dragged by his horse, it was unlikely the man was still alive, or if he was, that he would be able to cause trouble any time soon, but Titus didn't want to take a chance.

"Watch for that man who rode off," he told Miriam. "He might come back."

"If he does, what will you do?"

"Shoot him again," Titus answered. He knew there was a certain amount of bravado in that bold statement, but what else could he say?

He went on, "What did they say to you when they stopped you?"

"They asked me if I knew a man named Pike. I told them I didn't, but I don't think they believed me. Then they said he was an old man and that he would be on foot, and they said he'd probably been shot. I told them I hadn't seen anybody like that and then asked them what they were doing on Rancho Diablo land. I said that my pa wouldn't like them trespassing like that."

Despite the seriousness of the situation, Titus had to smile. "You really said that?" he asked. "To a couple of men like them?"

"Of course I did. I wasn't afraid of them." Miriam paused. "Well, I wasn't going to let them *see* that I was afraid of them, anyway."

Someday Miriam's fearlessness was going to get her in a lot of trouble, Titus thought. It nearly had today.

And it might yet if those two men had any friends nearby. He hadn't thought about until just now. There was no telling how many gunmen might be looking for them right this very minute.

"Come on," he said as he urged his horse to a slightly faster pace and tightened his grip on the wounded man. "Let's get back to the ranch."

5

Sometimes Sam Blaylock thought spring was his favorite season of the year. Of course, other times he thought the same thing about the other seasons. What it boiled down to today, he told himself as he sat at his desk and looked out the window, is that it was a beautiful day and he would have rather been outside doing almost anything than sitting here adding up a bunch of damn numbers and trying to make sense of them.

He got his excuse to forget about the paperwork a moment later when he saw Gabby Darbins hurrying toward the house from the direction of the barn. Gabby wasn't the sort of man to move fast unless something was wrong.

Sam stood up and went to the window, which was open because of the nice weather. Sam was a big man, and that became more apparent when he leaned over and stuck his head and shoulders out the window.

"Gabby!" he called. "Over here."

The ranch hand had been heading for the front door, but Sam motioned him toward the office window. Gabby changed direction and trotted over to him.

"Something wrong?" Sam asked.

Gabby was a little out of breath. He said, "Tucker spied Titus and Miss Miriam . . . comin' in the river trail. Said it looked like they had somebody with 'em. He grabbed a horse and rode out to meet 'em."

"Titus and Miriam are supposed to be working in the garden today. What in blazes are they doing out riding around?"

Even as he asked the question, Sam knew the answer, because he knew his children. Titus and Miriam had found some way to duck out of their chores and had gone off helling around again, the way they would all the time if Sam and Jenny didn't try to keep a tight rein on them.

"I dunno, boss," Gabby said. "I just – "

"Never mind," Sam said. "Tucker went to meet them, you say?"

"That's right."

That was a relief, anyway. Mike Tucker was young in years but ancient in experience and temperament. He was the steadiest man Sam knew and also the most dangerous, all at the same time. With Tucker around, the kids would be all right, even if they were bringing trouble home.

"Want me to saddle your horse?" Gabby asked as Sam drew back through the open window.

"No, they'll probably be here by the time I could get ready to ride." Sam turned away from the window. As he started out of the office, he paused long enough to pick up the coiled shell belt and holstered Smith & Wesson Model 3 .44 revolver he had placed on a chair earlier. He strapped the gunbelt around his hips.

Sam called to his wife as he strode to the front door. Jenny came out of the kitchen, her face flushed from cooking but to Sam's eyes as beautiful as ever. "What is it, Sam?" she asked. She was perceptive enough to have heard the promise of trouble in her husband's voice. The sight of Sam taking down his Henry rifle from the pegs near the front door must have confirmed that for her.

"Titus and Miriam are up to something again."

Jenny sighed in exasperation. "Those two! I swear, they're enough to drive a person to distraction."

"Or worse," Sam said. He stepped out onto the porch of the solidly built house. There were still a few things that needed to be done to finish it, but already it felt like home.

By the time he and Jenny reached the bottom of the steps, Gabby was there waiting for them. Elijah was with the old-timer. "I heard the commotion all the way out in the garden," he said. "What's wrong?"

"That's what we're going to find out as soon as your brother and sister get here," Sam told him.

They didn't have long to wait. Three horses appeared on the trail that led from the river. Sam recognized Miriam's paint and the horses Titus and Tucker rode. Titus's horse was in the middle, and there was somebody riding with him, propped up in the saddle while Titus rode behind and held him on the horse.

Jenny took hold of Sam's arm. "Dear Lord," she said. "Is that blood I see on that man riding with Titus?"

"It appears to be," Sam said. He gently disengaged his arm from his wife's grip and walked out to meet the riders, followed by Gabby.

Titus spoke first, saying excitedly, "Pa, I found this man up by the river – "

Sam held up a hand to stem what he knew would be a flood of words. "Is he shot?"

"Yeah, he's been wounded a couple of times. But he's still alive, and I think – "

"Gabby, let's get him down from there," Sam broke in again. There was something familiar about the wounded man, but Sam couldn't place him. As he and Gabby lifted the man down from the saddle, Sam glanced at Tucker and asked quietly, "Any trouble coming up behind them?"

Tucker shook his head. He was a slim man in his

twenties, with a close-cropped blond beard. "Not that I could see."

Sam was satisfied with that answer. If Tucker couldn't see something, chances were it wasn't there.

"Bring the man inside and put him on the sofa," Jenny said.

"He's liable to get blood on it," Sam warned.

"Miriam, run and get a blanket."

Miriam had already dismounted. She hurried to do as her mother said.

"Pa, I'm sorry about the chores – " Titus started to say.

Sam grunted a little as he and Gabby hefted the wounded man. If Duane had been here, he could have carried the man inside by himself without much trouble.

"We'll talk about that later," Sam said. "Right now, I want to hear about what happened, as soon as Gabby and I get this man inside."

The wounded man still looked familiar. Something stirred in Sam's memory, something from a long time in the past. But the name and the circumstances didn't come to him.

He and Gabby went up the steps and into the house with their burden. Gabby muttered under his breath about hefting and carrying and the damage it might be doing to his back. Miriam had fetched a blanket and spread it on the sofa. Carefully, they lowered the injured man onto it. Sam pushed the man's coat back and ripped his shirt open, revealing an ugly, blood-crusted bullet hole in his right side. Fresh blood still oozed from it.

Jenny said, "Titus, there's blood on your sleeve. Is it yours?"

"No, ma'am. It got on there while I was holdin' that fella on the horse."

Jenny nodded, satisfied that her son didn't have any injuries that needed tending. "Miriam, there's already hot water on the stove. Fetch a pan of it and some rags. Quickly. Sam, I'll need some whiskey."

Despite the seriousness of the situation, he said, "Need a swig to steady your nerves, eh?"

The look she gave him was anything but pleased. "I'll steady your nerves," she said. "You know I want it to clean this wound."

"Sorry," Sam said. "I'll get the bottle."

There was a bottle of whiskey in one of the drawers of his desk, kept there strictly for medicinal purposes, of course. When he came back with it, he found Jenny already cleaning some of the blood away from the wound with the rags and hot water Miriam had brought to her. Titus, Elijah, and Gabby stood by, watching as Jenny worked on the stranger. Tucker lounged in the doorway, facing out instead of in, his keen eyes scanning the landscape around the ranch headquarters.

Sam handed the whiskey to Jenny. Tucker looked around and said to him, "I might ought to take a ride up to the sawmill and let Duane and Randy know trouble might be circulating. Wouldn't want them to get taken by surprise."

Sam nodded. "That's a good idea. We'll be all right here."

As Tucker rode off, Sam told Gabby to wait on the porch and keep his eyes open. When the parlor was empty of everybody except the five members of the Blaylock family and the unconscious man, Sam looked at Titus and said, "Now, tell me what happened."

Titus did so, freely admitting that he had finagled Elijah into taking over his chores. He explained how he had found the wounded man in the brush and given him some water.

"He said he knew you, Pa," Titus went on. "He said he'd heard that his old friend Sam Blaylock had a ranch around here."

Jenny looked back over her shoulder. "Is that true, Sam?" she asked. "Do you know this man?"

"I'm sure I've seen him," Sam answered. "I feel like I ought to know who he is, but right now I can't come up with it."

Titus said, "I got him on my horse and started bringin' him back here, but then I saw Miriam – "

"What were you doing up there?" Sam asked his daughter.

"Looking for Titus so I could drag him back home," Miriam answered with her customary candor. "I was mad at him for ducking out of his chores. But then . . ."

Her normally feisty nature sort of deflated in front of Sam's eyes. "What is it?" he asked. "What happened?"

"These two men rode up and stopped me," Miriam answered. The words sounded like she had to force them out. Sam heard the sharp intake of breath from Jenny.

"Did they hurt you?" he asked in a voice as hard as granite.

"Oh, no, they just . . . they just scared me some. They wanted to know if I'd seen . . . him." She nodded toward the wounded man. "I told them I hadn't, but they didn't believe me. They knew he was wounded, so they must have been the ones who shot him."

"What for?"

Miriam shook her head. "I don't know. That's all they said, except to threaten me and say that they would make me tell the truth. Oh, and they said his name. Pike."

It was Sam's turn to draw in a sharp breath. He turned his head toward the sofa and stared down at the gray, haggard face of the unconscious man as memories came flooding back into his head. "My God, it *is* him," he said. "It's Orion Pike."

6

Arkansas

Sam Blaylock squinted through the smoke-hazed air of the tavern at the cards in his hand. He had three queens, and since he thought that was good enough to beat whatever Delbert Hardy had, he pushed a stack of coins into the center of the table.

"Raise it ten," Sam said.

Hardy was in his mid-twenties, six or seven years older than Sam. He had a round face, a thatch of muddy brown hair, and judging by his looks was as dumb as dirt. Sam might be young, but he already knew that a fella couldn't always go by appearances. Delbert Hardy was plenty cunning, and he was mean as sin on top of it.

"You're tryin' to bluff me, boy," Hardy said. "I'll just see your damn ten and bump it five more, how about that?"

Sam tried to sound confident as he said, "If you want to throw away good money after bad, that's your business, Delbert."

Hardy scowled. The game had been going on all afternoon, and Sam had won consistently, taking mostly small pots. They added up, though, and by now Sam had a considerable amount of Hardy's money in the pile in front of him. Hardy had a high opinion of himself as a poker player and didn't like losing.

What he didn't know was that he had half a dozen different tells that Sam had been able to spot. Hardy prided himself on his poker face but didn't seem to notice all the other little things he did that gave away what kind of hand he had.

"Well, what are you gonna do?" Hardy prodded. This hand was down to just the two of them. The other players had dropped out one by one as the betting went around the table.

"I believe I'll see your five," Sam said as he pushed in the coins, "and raise another twenty."

He thought for a second Hardy was going to pop, the man got so red-faced. Hardy said, "By God, I call!" and shoved forward the money to back it up. He slapped his cards down on the table. "Beat three jacks!"

"All right, I will," Sam said as he laid his own hand face-up.

Hardy's eyes bulged from their sockets as he saw the three queens looking up at him. He started to bolt from his chair and as his hand moved toward the pistol tucked behind his belt he said, "You damn little – "

That was as far as he got before the tip of Sam's Arkansas toothpick poked through the fabric of his homespun shirt and pricked his belly.

"I can have your guts spilling out on this table before you can draw and cock that pistol, Delbert," Sam said with a tone of quiet menace in his voice. "But you go right ahead and try it if you want to. I figure you were just about to call me a cheater, and I don't cotton to that."

Hardy swallowed hard and tried for some bluster. "Put that pigsticker away, boy, or I'll take it away from you and make you damned sorry you ever pulled it."

"I don't think so. I beat you fair and square, Delbert. The sooner you realize that, the better."

"I never said you were cheatin'."

"You thought it," Sam said.

Hardy moved his hand well away from the pistol and said, "Forget it. I ain't gonna waste my time on some kid." He sneered. "I got better things to do."

"Fine. Go do 'em."

"I will!"

Hardy took a step back away from the knife and turned to stalk toward the door. Sam kept a close eye on him as Hardy left the tavern. If the man was thinking about turning suddenly and trying some sort of fast draw, Sam was ready. He had put in long hours practicing with the knife, and he could bury it in Hardy's chest with a quick throw before Hardy could get a shot off.

Sam was betting that he could, anyway. He knew the stakes might be his life.

Hardy left the tavern without turning around. Sam gathered in the pot. One of the other players asked, "You still in, Sam?"

Sam shook his head as he stacked up his winnings and distributed them in his pockets. "I don't think so," he said. "My pa's expecting me back. He sent me to town to do a little horse-trading." He grinned. "I'll just have to tell him I wasn't able to make any deals today."

Sam left the tavern, which was a sturdy log building on an isolated stretch of road that twisted through the Ozarks. The thickly wooded slopes of the mountains loomed in all directions.

The saddle mule Sam had ridden into the settlement was tied in front of the tavern. Sam freed the reins and mounted. He turned the mule to the north and rode for a couple of hundred yards, traveling around a sharp bend in the trail, before he brought the animal to a halt and waited.

A few minutes later he heard the thud of hoofbeats. Another rider rounded the bend in the trail. He was a slender man in his late thirties whose dark hair was already graying. He lifted a hand in greeting as he rode up to Sam and reined in. Anybody who had been paying attention in the tavern might have recognized him. He'd been standing at the bar, nursing a beer, while Sam played cards with Delbert Hardy and the other men.

"Looks like you did pretty good, Sam," he said now.

"Thanks to everything you taught me, Orion," Sam replied. He took some of the money he had won out of his pocket. "Here's your share, like we agreed."

"You don't have to do that," Orion Pike replied with a smile.

"Yes, I do," Sam insisted. "You taught me what to look for. I couldn't have taken Hardy like I did without your help. You earned it."

Pike chuckled and reached out to take the money. "In that case . . . I'm much obliged."

The two of them began riding along the road side by side. Sam knew that if anybody saw them and later told his folks that he'd been hanging around Orion Pike, his pa would skin him alive. Pike was rumored to be a pretty shady character. People in this neck of the woods said that he was a smuggler and a thief, and it was whispered that he had killed a couple of men, too, one over a debt and the other over a woman. The thing of it was, nothing had ever been proven against him, and as he had pointed out to Sam on more than on occasion, once a fella got a reputation, folks blamed him for everything bad that happened, even when he didn't have anything to do with it.

"You know, you're a smart lad, Sam," Pike said now. "You picked up on what I was tellin' you right away. You might have a real future, son."

"You mean as a smuggler?" Sam asked. He couldn't keep the excitement out of his voice. He was young enough that breaking the law seemed daring and glamorous to him, at least as long as nobody really got hurt.

"Aw, now, who said anything about smugglin'?" Pike laughed. "All my business deals are strictly on the up-and-up."

Sam smiled. "Whatever you say, Orion."

"Anyway," Pike went on, "I'm thinkin' that was I to take a smart young fella like you under my wing, there's a whole lot I could teach – Ah, hell."

"What is it?"

"We got somebody followin' us."

Sam twisted in the saddle to look back. Sure enough, about eighty yards behind them a couple of riders moved briskly along the trail. They were too far away for Sam to get a good look at them, but he thought he recognized the big roan horse that Delbert Hardy always rode.

Fear jolted through Sam. Hardy had quite a few friends around here who were almost as mean as he was. Everybody knew that Hardy didn't like to lose. Beating him in front of the folks in the tavern like that would just make him madder.

"We'd better get out of here," Sam said.

"Sounds like a good idea to me," Orion Pike agreed. He kicked his horse into a run, and Sam followed suit with the mule.

As the animals pounded along the trail, Sam twisted his head to look behind them. The men who were following them had increased their pace, too, and now were galloping hard after him and Pike.

"Orion, this might be bad!" Sam called over the thundering hoofbeats.

"No might be about it!" Pike shot back. Hearing the alarm in the older man's voice, Sam jerked back around again and saw two more riders emerge from some rocks at the side of the road. They charged toward Sam and Pike, and a second later Sam heard the dull boom of a gunshot and saw smoke and flame gush from the muzzle of a pistol fired by one of the men in front of them.

7

Thick forest crowded up on both sides of the road. Sam thought maybe he and Pike could abandon their mounts and take to the trees on foot. With a little luck, they might be able to elude the men who wanted to kill them.

But instead of fleeing, Pike yanked a brace of pistols from under his coat, yelled, "Follow me, boy!" and met the charge head-on, galloping toward the men in front of them.

Sam followed the older man, bending forward in his saddle so he'd be a smaller target. What sounded like a rifle went off somewhere behind them. Something hummed past his ear. With a sick feeling in his stomach, he realized it was a rifle ball. A few inches to the right and it would have blown his brains out.

The gap between Orion Pike and the men attacking from the front seemed to close in a heartbeat. The men had to veer their horses apart to keep Pike's mount from crashing into them. As they split up, Pike flashed between them. Both pistols came up and geysered flame. One of the men screamed and went out of the saddle. Sam saw the man crash to the ground as he galloped past.

He saw how half the man's face was blown away in a bloody mess, too, and he knew it was a sight he would never forget.

Behind them, Delbert Hardy howled curses and kept coming, even as his friends fell back. With one man dead and another wounded, the third man probably figured this wasn't as much sport as he'd thought it would be.

Hardy wasn't going to give up, though, Sam saw as he looked back over his shoulder. Hardy had a long-barreled flintlock rifle in one hand, the reins in the other, and flapped his elbows like the wings of a big, ugly bird as he galloped after his quarry.

Up ahead of Sam, Orion Pike had reached the rocks where the bushwhackers had hidden. He rode among them and swung down from the saddle, taking his rifle with him. He waved an arm at Sam and shouted, "Get out of the way!"

Sam pulled his mule to the other side of the road and watched as Pike laid the barrel of his rifle over the top of a rock and sighted down it. Delbert Hardy must have realized at that moment where his anger and pride had led him. He hauled back on the reins and tried to slow his horse so he could turn, but he was too late. Pike had already drawn a bead on him.

Pike's rifle blasted.

Hardy went backward out of the saddle as if he'd been punched by a giant fist. He landed in the road on his back, with his arms and legs outflung. His back arched for a moment as a death spasm went through him, then he sagged into the dirt and didn't move again.

Sam's mule had come to a stop when he quit banging his heels into its flanks. Sam sat there looking down the road at the two bodies lying sprawled in it. He had been in fights before, but he had never seen anybody shot down like that.

Hardy's other two friends were nowhere in sight.

Pike was busy reloading his rifle when Sam looked

over at him. Matter of factly, Pike set the rifle aside when he was finished and started reloading his pistols. He grinned at Sam and said, "When you're in a fight, use every chance you get to reload your guns. You don't know when you'll get another chance."

"You . . . you killed them." Sam's voice sounded strange to his ears.

"And what do you think they planned to do to you, boy? You don't know Delbert Hardy as well as I do. He's killed men before, over less than beatin' him at cards in front of his friends."

"You knew that, and you let me play him anyway?"

Pike's shoulders rose and fell. "Nobody made you sit down at that table. Anyway, I planned to keep an eye on you, to make sure you stayed safe. I feel a certain responsibility, you know."

"The sheriff's going to come after us for this."

"For what? Defending ourselves?" Pike laughed. "Here's another lesson for you, Sammy. Worry about what you need to get done, not about the law. It'll just get in the way of what's necessary."

"What are we going to do about the bodies?"

"Not a damn thing. Hardy's friends will come back for them." Pike grinned as he mounted up. "We've already done our part. Now, let's get you home . . ."

#

Rancho Diablo

"You know this man, Sam?" Jenny asked as Sam looked down at the wounded man on the sofa in his parlor.

Slowly, Sam nodded. "I know him. At least, I used to a long time ago. When I was a kid in the Ozarks, not a man full-grown yet. He . . . helped me out of a bad scrape once."

He started to explain about the poker game and Delbert Hardy, then realized his children were standing right there listening to him and thought better of it. They didn't need to hear how foolish their father had been as a young man. To be fair, he thought, Titus and

Miriam came by some of their wild, reckless nature honestly.

"Well, then, I suppose I'm glad Titus and Miriam were able to help him," Jenny said. "Although we're going to have a talk, Titus, about you trying to take advantage of your brother's good heart, and you, young lady, about riding off that way without telling anyone where you're going."

"Yes, ma'am," both of them muttered.

"Do you think he's going to be all right?" Sam asked.

"Judging by the stains on his shirt, and on Titus's, he's lost quite a bit of blood. But the bullet went straight through, so he's lucky it's not still in him. If the wounds are kept clean and he gets a lot of rest, he should stand a good chance of recovering."

Sam nodded. "Good. Once you've finished patching him up, I'll get Duane from the sawmill and we'll move him out to the bunkhouse."

Jenny glanced up at him. "We could put him in the boys' room if you'd like, Sam. I'm sure they wouldn't mind sleeping in the bunkhouse."

"No," Sam said. "I'd rather Orion be out there."

"Orion Pike, you said his name is? I don't recall you ever speaking of him."

"No, I don't suppose I ever did."

Sam's mind went back to those far-off days again. Despite what Pike had said, he worried that the sheriff would arrest them for killing Hardy and the other man. But nothing was ever said about it, and Sam realized a few days later that the bodies hadn't been found. He suspected that Pike had gone back out there and disposed of them somehow.

But that left the other two men. They could go to the law and tell what happened.

Only they dropped out of sight, too. And with every day that passed, Sam became more convinced that they were lying in a shallow grave somewhere, their throats cut. Pike had made sure the law wouldn't come after them.

Of course, he'd been protecting himself more than Sam, who, when you came right down to it, hadn't fired a shot. But he was the one Hardy had been after, so he figured he bore a share of the blame for the killings, too.

After that Sam hadn't spent as much time with Orion Pike as before. Their friendship waned, and one day Sam realized that he hadn't seen Pike for a long time. The man had simply disappeared from that part of the Ozarks.

Sam wasn't sorry that Pike was gone. He felt considerable obligation – Pike had saved his life, no doubt about that – but traveling the same trails as Pike would have led him straight into more trouble sooner or later. No doubt about that, either.

Sam turned to look at Titus and Miriam. "What else happened out there?" he asked. "Where are those other men, the ones who bothered you, Miriam?"

Both of the kids looked uncomfortable, and Sam knew he hadn't heard the worst of it yet. Titus looked down at the floor and said, "Mr. Pike . . . well, he shot one of them."

"Dear Lord!" Jenny said. "He *shot* someone?"

"That's right, Ma. He had to, to save Miriam. But then he passed out again and the other fella started up the hill at us and he was shooting and I . . . I . . ."

"What did you *do*, son?" Sam asked.

Titus swallowed hard. "I shot him, Pa."

8

Sam drew his Henry rifle and laid it across the saddle in front of him. He didn't know what they were riding into, and he wanted to be ready for trouble.

Mike Tucker rode beside him. Tucker hadn't brought along a rifle, but he carried three Tranter revolvers, one on each hip and another holstered at the small of his back. The double-action .450 caliber revolvers held five rounds apiece, giving Tucker fifteen shots before he had to reload, the same number of shots Sam carried in the Henry. Tucker was so fast that at close range he could create a veritable hailstorm of lead with those Tranters.

Titus brought up the rear behind Sam and Tucker. Jenny hadn't wanted him to come along, but Sam had insisted. If the boy was old enough to go around shooting folks, he was old enough to take some responsibility for it. Besides, Titus could show them exactly where the ruckus had taken place. Sam wanted to take a look at the dead man and see if he recognized *him*, too.

Once he'd heard about the shooting, Sam hadn't waited for Jenny to finish doctoring Orion Pike. He'd sent Gabby to the sawmill to fetch Duane and Randy.

Duane could move Pike to the bunkhouse, and then he, Randy, and Gabby would watch over the place. A threat to Rancho Diablo and the Blaylock family could be lurking up here along the river, and if it was, Sam wanted to know about it as soon as possible.

The three of them rode through a stand of trees into an open field. Titus said, "He's over there."

Sam reined in and looked where his son was pointing. He saw the dark shape on the ground. The body didn't quite look human anymore with all the life gone out of it.

"Stay here," he said to Titus. "Keep your eyes open."

"Yes, sir."

Sam and Tucker rode toward the dead man, taking their time about it now. There was no hurry. The hombre wasn't going anywhere.

And his wounded friend hadn't come back for him. That meant something, Sam thought. If there had been more of the hardcases nearby, they would have retrieved the corpse by now.

The man lay on his back. The crimson flower of blood on his shirt front had dried to an ugly brown splotch. He had lost his hat, and his face and head were pretty beaten up from being dragged by his horse.

Sam was pretty sure he had never seen the man before, but he dismounted to take a closer look. "You know him, Tucker?"

"Nope," Tucker said. "Don't like the looks of him, though, even dead."

Sam knew what Tucker meant. The coarse features and the beard-stubbled jaw and cheeks gave the man an air of brutality. The thought of a man like this grabbing his daughter made anger surge up inside Sam. At this moment, he was thankful that Orion Pike had been here to shoot the varmint.

"His horse is over yonder," Tucker commented. "Want me to fetch him?"

"Yeah, do that," Sam said. "We'll need the horse to carry him back to the ranch."

"What are you gonna with him?"

Sam looked down at the corpse. "Take him to town, I guess. Marshall Tolliver might recognize him, or at least have some paper on him."

While Tucker went to get the dead man's horse, Sam waved Titus over. The boy rode up looking like he wished he was almost anywhere else. His eyes avoided the man on the ground.

"Where did the other one go?" Sam asked. "The one you shot."

Titus pointed. "Into those trees over there."

"Could you tell how bad he was hit?"

"No, sir, not really. He grabbed his shoulder, and when he rode off he was sort of leaning in that direction."

Sam nodded. "Could have been anything from a crease to a busted bone. I'll go have a look. It's possible he could still be over there in the trees. He might've fallen off his horse and bled to death."

"What . . . what do you want me to do?"

"Stay here and help Tucker get this man across his saddle."

Titus looked pale and a little sick. Sam knew he was being rough on the boy. Titus shouldn't have been up here in the first place, though.

But on the other hand, if Titus hadn't come along and found Orion Pike, Pike would probably be dead by now. And since Sam owed Pike his life, he couldn't help but be glad that Titus had been able to help him.

Sam rode up on the hillside where Titus had wounded the second man and spotted a splash of dried blood on the grass. He saw more blood drops scattered here and there as he rode toward the trees where the man had disappeared. Nobody was around. Sam didn't know whether the man was still alive or not, but he hadn't died here.

By the time Sam got back to the place where he had left Titus, Tucker had returned with the dead man's horse. Together, he and Titus had hoisted the corpse onto the animal's back and draped it face-down over the saddle. Tucker tied the dead man's hands and feet together under the horse's belly to keep him from slipping off.

"Let's go home," Sam said.

With Tucker leading the dead man's horse, they rode back to the ranch house. Worry still stirred restlessly in Sam's brain. He wished he knew whether the two men searching for Pike had been alone.

When they got back, Duane Beatty came out of the house to greet them. He was a tall, heavily-muscled man with dark hair and a boisterous nature. Duane was the sort who always found the fun that life had to offer, even when it meant taking reckless chances, but he could be serious, too, when he needed to.

Such as a moment like this. He nodded toward the corpse and said, "I reckon that's him?"

"It is," Sam said. "Where is everybody?"

"Gabby and Randy are in the bunkhouse with the old-timer. I've been staying in the house with the missus and the youngsters."

Sam nodded. "Good. I want somebody in the house with them all the time until we're sure there's not going to be any more trouble. You and Tucker can take turns."

"Gabby told me what happened. You think the man Titus shot has friends?"

"I expect we'll find out sooner or later," Sam said.

He motioned for Titus to follow him in the house. Jenny, Miriam, and Elijah were sitting in the parlor. The blanket that had been placed on the sofa to protect it from Orion Pike's blood was gone. Sam didn't know whether Jenny would try to wash it or just burn it.

"Did you find the man, Sam?" Jenny asked. She had been pretty shaken up when she found out that Titus had been mixed up in a gunfight and had shot a man, but she seemed calmer now.

"We did," Sam replied with a nod. "He's outside on his horse. I'll take the body into town and see if Marshal

Tolliver knows anything about him. But before I do that . . ." He turned to face Titus. "What did you promise Elijah when you got him to take over your work in the garden today?"

"Uh . . . that I would do his chores for a week."

"All right. You'll keep your promise. And then you'll do his chores for another week as punishment."

Titus's eyes widened.

Sam held up a hand to stop him from saying anything. "Save your complaints. That's not all. Unless me or your mother tells you to get on a horse to run some errand, you won't be riding anywhere for those two weeks, either." He looked over at Miriam. "The same goes for you, young lady."

"But Pa, I didn't try to take advantage of Elijah," she argued. "I just went looking for Titus."

"Instead of doing your own work," Sam said. "That's it. No riding unless one of us tells you to. But at least you don't have extra chores."

Miriam sank back in the armchair where she was sitting and pouted. That didn't bother Sam. He looked at Jenny and saw the little nod she gave him, indicating that she agreed with the punishment he had handed out.

"I'll bet your pa wouldn't have been so hard on you," Titus muttered as Sam started toward the door.

Sam paused. "Boy, my pa would have blistered my hide if – "

If he knew that I'd been hanging around with Orion Pike and almost got myself shot because of it.

"Never mind," Sam said as he opened the door. "I'm going to take that body to town."

9

The settlement of Shooter's Cross was a couple of miles downstream and on the other side of the Brazos from Rancho Diablo. A tall, skinny, white-bearded old-timer named Eustace Kendall owned and operated the ferry that carried passengers, horses, and freight across the river. When Sam rode up leading the dead man's horse, Eustace was sitting on a stool on the short dock that stuck out into the river.

The ferryman leaned over and spat a brown stream of tobacco juice into the Brazos. "Got another dead one, eh?" he asked.

"It's not like I've got a corpse with me every time I go to town," Sam said.

"No, but it happens often enough it don't surprise me no more." Eustace put his hands on his knees and pushed himself to his feet. "Who's this one?"

"Don't know. That's what I'm hoping to find out."

"You shoot him?"

"Nope." Sam decided it might be prudent not to go into too much detail just yet. Eustace was something of a gossip. "Found his body in a field north of my place." That was true, as far as it went.

"Is that blood on his shirt?"

"It is."

Eustace's head bobbed in a nod, reinforcing his somewhat bird-like appearance. "Got himself shot, then, did he?"

"That's what it looks like," Sam said. "I'm taking the body to Marshal Tolliver. He can figure out what to do with it."

Eustace began taking down the poles on the side of the ferry that was tied to the dock. "Come aboard," he invited. "Since you been around here, I'm startin' to feel this is more like the Styx than the Brazos. But which side is Hell?"

"That's a good question," Sam said.

The river was pretty wide here, at least for Texas, where major rivers would be counted as creeks in some parts of the country. Eustace might look scrawny, but he had been operating the ferry for a long time and had no trouble hauling it from one side of the river to the other. Sam paid for his passage and disembarked on the other bank to continue his grim errand.

The town ran along the river bank for about a dozen blocks and extended several blocks away from the river on land that had been cleared of its thick natural forest. Because lumber was abundant, most of the buildings were of frame construction, but there were some rock and brick structures, too. Shooter's Cross was growing, and some of the population often gathered at the ferry landing when Eustace Kendall brought somebody across. Sam supposed folks happened to be busy today, though, because only one man stood on the bank near the dock, watching him lead the other horse with its grisly burden off the ferry.

Unfortunately, that man was just about the last person Sam wanted to see today.

"Hello, Blaylock," Mitchell McCarthy greeted him. The stocky, bearded newspaperman nodded toward the corpse and went on, "Someone else you've killed?"

Even though they usually kept up a semi-polite

façade, Sam and McCarthy didn't like each other, and both men knew it. McCarthy owned the local newspaper, had his fingers in several other businesses, and as far as Sam was concerned was a pretty shady character despite his self-imposed air of respectability. Even though he couldn't prove it, Sam was convinced McCarthy had set some outlaws on him a while back, when Sam was carrying a considerable amount of money he had won from McCarthy in a poker game.

"I never laid eyes on this fella until after he was dead," Sam said. "I'm doing the legal, responsible thing and turning his body over to the authorities."

McCarthy stuck his hands in his pockets and asked bluntly, "Who killed him?"

"That's a good question. I didn't see it happen. I just found the body on my land."

McCarthy's eyes glittered. He had to realize that Sam was evading the truth. He opened his mouth to say something else, but before he could, Sam hitched the horses into motion and said, "I've got to get to the marshal's office." McCarthy had to step aside quickly to get out of the way. Sam heard some muttering behind him but didn't look back.

The marshal's office was a squarish, one-story stone building next to a feed store. Everett Tolliver stepped out of the office just as Sam rode up. The lawman was built like a blacksmith, but he had a certain degree of fastidiousness about his appearance. Always carefully shaved and barbered, he wore dark, sober suits and a black hat. Sam liked him, but the two of them didn't really know each other all that well yet, so there was still some wariness between them.

Tolliver didn't look pleased as he asked, "Is that a body on that horse, Sam?"

"I believe you've seen enough of them to recognize one when you see it, Everett," Sam replied.

"Who is it this time?"

"I was hoping you could tell me." Sam started to dismount. "I'll get him off of there."

Tolliver stopped him by stepping forward and raising a hand. "Leave him right where he is. I don't need a dead man cluttering up my office. Take him down to the undertaker's. I'll have a look at him there." Tolliver paused. "Oh, by the way . . . did you kill him?"

"Nope. And I'm not sure why everybody just assumes that I did."

Tolliver just grunted, as if the answer to that should have been obvious.

"Did I catch you going out on some errand?" Sam asked as he rode along Main Street with Tolliver walking beside him.

"Actually, I was just going over to the café for a piece of pie. I'm feeling a mite peckish, and it's a while yet until suppertime."

"I'm sorry to interfere with that."

Tolliver waved a hand. "Don't worry about it. I probably didn't need the pie anyway."

They reached the undertaking establishment run by Joshua Shadrack and went around to the back. Live people went in the front door at Shadrack's, dead ones in the back. The sound of hammering greeted them, so Sam wasn't surprised when they found the burly undertaker putting together a coffin. Several more were stacked on the building's back porch.

"We've got some work for you, Joshua," Tolliver said.

Shadrack set his hammer aside. He was a large, bald man. His shirtsleeves were rolled up, revealing forearms that bulged with muscle. He looked at Sam and asked, "Your doing, Mr. Blaylock?"

Sam didn't try to hold in the impatient sigh that came from him. "No," he said.

"Well, let's take him inside."

Sam and Shadrack carried the dead man inside and placed him on a table in the room where the undertaker prepared bodies for burial.

"Is he a friend of yours?" Shadrack asked.

"Never saw him before today."

Shadrack looked at the marshal. "Is the town paying

for my services?"

"Not hardly," Tolliver answered without hesitation. He looked carefully at the dead man for a moment and went on, "He's not from around here, and he didn't die in town, so I don't see why the town should have to pay for putting him in the ground."

"I'll pay for it," Sam said, then as he remembered how this man had treated Miriam, he added, "Just nothing fancy or expensive."

Shadrack nodded in understanding. "What's the deceased's name?"

Sam looked at Tolliver. The marshal shook his head and said, "I don't know him, Sam. I'm like you. I never saw him before."

"Why don't we go back to your office and talk about this?"

"That's just what I was about to suggest."

10

When they got back to the marshal's office, Tolliver hung his hat on a nail and offered Sam a cup of coffee from the pot that sat on a wood-burning stove in the corner. "It's pretty potent," he warned.

"Good," Sam said. "I can use it."

Tolliver filled tin cups for both of them and waved Sam into a leather armchair in front of the desk. He sat down in a similar chair behind the desk.

"I reckon you'd better tell me about it. You didn't just come across that man's body on your ranch, did you?"

"Actually, my boy Titus found him," Sam said, once again deciding it might be wise to withhold some of the details. He didn't like lying to Everett Tolliver, because he wanted to be friends with the lawman, but until he found out what was going on, he was going to give Orion Pike the benefit of the doubt and keep Pike's name out of it. "I thought maybe we could look through the wanted posters you've got and see if we could find him."

"What makes you think he's an outlaw?"

"Call it a hunch."

Tolliver nodded. "I have hunches, too, sometimes. Like right now, I've got a hunch there's more to this than you're telling me, Sam. But I know what you mean about that fellow. He looked like the sort who might have been in trouble with the law." Tolliver leaned over and opened a drawer in the desk. He brought out a large stack of papers and thrust them toward Sam. "Help yourself."

Sam took the wanted posters and began going through them. Some had drawings of the outlaws on them, some only descriptions. Sam found a few he thought might have been the man Pike had shot, but he wasn't sure. Then, toward the bottom of the stack, he came across a poster with a drawing of a hard, brutal face on it that seemed to leap up at him. The artist had done a good job working from a description. Sam was certain the man in the picture was the same one who was now lying cold and lifeless in Joshua Shadrack's back room.

"This is him," he said as he tossed the reward dodger onto the desk in front of Everett Tolliver.

The marshal leaned forward in his chair to pick up the paper. He looked at it for a full minute before he nodded. "I think you're right. Jonah Trent," he read. "Wanted for bank robbery, train robbery, and murder in Texas, Louisiana, Arkansas, and Missouri. Sounds like a pretty bad hombre. Says here he's supposed to be a member of a gang that's been raising hell in those four states ever since the end of the war." Tolliver looked up from the reward poster and locked his gaze with Sam's. "What was he doing on Rancho Diablo?"

Sam met Tolliver's intense look with one of his own. "You'd have to ask him, Marshal," he said, "and I don't think he's going to answer."

Tolliver grunted. "No, I guess not." He tapped the paper. "What about this gang Trent rode with? Have you seen any other suspicious characters around your spread?"

"No, I haven't," Sam said, which, strictly speaking, was true.

The news that the dead man was part of a gang of

outlaws made a chill go down Sam's spine. Certainly it was possible that Trent had split off from the gang and had been traveling only with the man Titus had shot. But it was equally likely that a number of other dangerous hombres were out there somewhere close, maybe even on Rancho Diablo at this very minute. Suddenly Sam wanted more than anything else to get home.

Sam came to his feet and said, "At least we know who he was, even if we don't know why he was in these parts. I'll be riding – "

"Wait a minute," Tolliver said. He stood up as well. "You can't just leave, Sam."

Nothing was going to keep Sam away from his family short of being locked up in the marshal's jail, and Sam didn't think that was going to happen, no matter what Tolliver did. He started to say, "Everett, don't – "

Tolliver interrupted by tapping a finger on the wanted poster again and saying, "According to this, there's a five hundred dollar reward for Trent, dead or alive. He's dead and you brought him in, so I reckon that bounty belongs to you. I'll put in the claim for you, if you'd like."

Sam hadn't even thought about the possibility of a reward, so the marshal's offer came as a surprise to him. He didn't really have to consider it, though. He just shook his head and said, "No. I didn't kill him, and even if I had, I wouldn't want any blood money."

"You're sure?"

"Positive."

Tolliver shrugged. "All right. I'm not going to put in for it, either, so I suppose the reward will go unclaimed. You really ought to take it, though, Sam. You told Joshua you'd pay for burying Trent. A man who's saving up to buy cattle doesn't need that sort of unexpected expense."

"Maybe not, but I'll stand for it." Sam gave the lawman a curt nod and left the office before Tolliver could say anything else.

He wasn't happy to see Mitchell McCarthy standing

in the street outside, as if the newspaperman had been waiting for him to emerge. McCarthy said, "Were you able to identify the dead man?"

Sam jerked his head toward the door as he untied his horse from the hitch rack. "You'll have to ask the marshal about that."

"Don't worry, I intend to," McCarthy said with a smug smile. "I've just been talking to Joshua Shadrack. His business has really boomed since you came here, Blaylock. Now there's been yet another killing you're mixed up in."

"I'm not mixed up in anything," Sam said. "I just brought in the body."

"Maybe we'll let the readers of the newspaper make up their own minds about that."

Anger welled up inside Sam. He was already thought of by many of the citizens in Shooter's Cross as a wild, dangerous man who was one step removed from being an outlaw. The fact that he was a family man, a hard worker who had built a sawmill and was well on his way to turning an old, abandoned ranch into a going concern, didn't seem to have any bearing on the way people felt about him. They saw the gun on his hip and knew he had killed several men, and that was all they needed to know to form an opinion about him. It wasn't a good opinion, either. A few folks seemed willing to give him a chance, but McCarthy was bound and determined to turn them against him, too.

Going after the newspaperman right here on Main Street, in broad daylight, wouldn't help matters, either. It would just prove McCarthy's point. So Sam got a tight rein on his temper and said, "You write whatever you want to, McCarthy. I trust people to be able to figure out the truth."

McCarthy laughed. He spoke quietly, and no one was close enough to hear him except Sam when he said, "Then you're naïve. People believe what I tell them to believe."

Sam didn't say anything. He swung up into the

saddle and rode toward the river without looking back at McCarthy, but inside he was still angry.

"Get that body delivered?" Eustace asked when Sam reached the ferry.

"Yeah, and now I'm going home."

He hoped everything was still all right when he got there.

11

It was late in the afternoon by the time Sam reached Rancho Diablo. With everything that had been going on, he had missed lunch and his stomach was growling. He had more important things to worry about than being hungry, though.

As Sam rode up to the barn, Gabby Darbins stepped out with a shotgun in his hands. "Heard somebody comin' and hoped it was you, Sam," Gabby said.

Sam dismounted. "Anything happen while I was gone?"

"Nope. It's been downright peaceful. Tucker's in the house right now, Duane and Randy in the bunkhouse with that fella Pike. He's awake again and been wantin' to talk to you."

"I want to talk to him, too," Sam said.

Instead of heading straight to the bunkhouse, though, he went to the house first. He found Jenny and Tucker in the kitchen. Tucker was sitting at the table peeling potatoes. Even engaged in such an innocent domestic chore, he looked a little like a big cat ready to spring at his prey.

Jenny left the stove and came over to put a hand on

Sam's arm. "Did you find out who that man was?" she asked quietly.

"Yeah. His name was Jonah Trent."

"A wanted man?" Tucker asked without looking up from the spud he was peeling.

"That's right. Rode with a gang that's wanted all over this part of the country for bank robbery and such."

Tucker nodded. "I figured as much."

"What about the rest of the outlaws?" Jenny asked. "They're bound to be around here somewhere, aren't they?"

"Not necessarily," Sam said. "The reward poster I saw was dated a while back. Trent could have split with the others. Or he could still be part of the gang. We just don't know."

Jenny's mouth was a tight line as she asked, "What about Mr. Pike? Is he one of them, too?"

"I don't know that, either. Thought I'd go ask him."

"When you knew him before, Sam . . . was he an outlaw?" "Some said he was, or the next thing to it, anyway," Sam admitted. "But he saved my life one time, Jenny. I owe him for that. I'm not going to think the worst of him until I see the proof of it with my own eyes, or until he tells me himself."

She squeezed his arm. "All right. I understand that. But Sam . . . I'm glad you had Duane take him out to the bunkhouse. I wouldn't really feel comfortable with a man like that under the same roof as the children."

Sam nodded to let her know that he understood. He felt the same way.

As Sam started toward the door, Tucker asked, "You want me to come with you?"

Sam managed to smile. "No, I wouldn't want to take you away from that important work you're doing."

Orion Pike was propped up in one of the bunks when Sam walked in a couple of minutes later after passing Duane and Randy sitting on the steps outside. Bandages were wrapped around Pike's midsection to hold the dressings in place on his wounds, and his leg sported a bandage where a bullet had nicked him, too. A grin wreathed his leathery face as he said, "Sam! Is it really you?"

"It's me, all right." Sam extended his hand and shook with the old-timer. He used his foot to draw a stool over by the bunk, sat down, and dropped his hat on the foot of the mattress. "I figured I'd never see you again, Orion. It's been a long time."

"A hell of a long time," Pike agreed. "You figured I was dead, didn't you?"

Sam shrugged. "The thought crossed my mind." He added in a dry tone, "You did seem to live sort of dangerous-like. Judging by the shape you're in now, that hasn't changed much."

"That's the truth. But I'd be a lot worse off if not for that boy of yours, Sam. He's a real humdinger! One of those hands of yours told me the boy shot that other fella who was after me."

Sam didn't have to ask which of the ranch hands had told Pike about what Titus had done. Gabby hadn't acquired that nickname for no good reason.

"I want to ask you about those fellas, Orion, if you feel up to talking – "

"Say, do you remember those times we spent together up in the Ozarks? Those were mighty fine days, I swear. For a while there I had high hopes you and me would team up. You were always smart as a whip, Sam. We would've rode high, wide, and handsome, yes, sir!"

"You might be right about that . . . but that sort of got fouled up when Delbert Hardy and his friends tried to kill us."

A solemn look came over Pike's face. "You remember that day, do you?"

"I don't reckon I'll ever forget it," Sam said. "First time a shot came close enough to my ear I heard it go past."

"Bet you've heard a few bullets since then, haven't you?"

"More than I like to think about." Sam wanted to get

down to business. "I just got back from Shooter's Cross. I took the body of the man you shot to the marshal there."

"You did, did you?" Pike gave him a sly look. "Did that lawman know who he was?"

"No, but we found his picture on one of the marshal's wanted posters. His name was Jonah Trent . . . but you already knew that, didn't you, Orion?"

Pike sighed. "I'd be a plumb fool if I didn't know who was tryin' to kill me, now wouldn't I?"

Sam didn't answer that. Instead he said, "According to the wanted poster, Trent rides with a gang that's been holding up banks and such from here to Missouri. You know anything about that, Orion?"

Anger flashed in the old man's eyes. "What do you want me to say, Sam? That I didn't know those fellas and they came after me for no good reason?"

"What was their reason?" Sam's voice was hard as he went on, "Are you part of their gang?"

"Blast it, no! I'm not." Pike sat up straighter as he spoke. He grimaced as if the movement made a twinge of pain go through him. "Leastways, I'm not anymore."

"But you were." It wasn't a question this time.

Pike sighed. "Listen, Sam, it's been a hard life. You think I wanted to spend it skalleyhootin' around, gettin' in one scrape after another? I wanted to settle down, too, to have a home and a family like you got here. You don't know how happy I was for you when I heard some soldiers in a saloon talkin' about how you'd started this ranch. Reckon they knew you from your scoutin' days. I figured that even if I couldn't have this sort of life, you deserved it."

"Why didn't you settle down?"

A smile appeared on Pike's weathered face again. "I reckon I was always just a mite too fond of whiskey and cards and shady women. And to tell you the truth, honest work and me never seemed to get along that well. What we think we want out of life and what we're cut out for ain't always the same thing."

Sam clasped his hands together and leaned forward on the stool. "This is your long-winded way of saying that you and Trent were part of the same gang?"

"Yeah. Ain't no point in denyin' it, I suppose."

"And there was some sort of falling out among the gang?"

Pike scratched at his lean, gray-stubbled jaw. "Not exactly. I'm the one who fell out, I guess you could say."

"So the whole bunch is after you?" That was about the worst news he could have heard, Sam thought.

"Listen, Sam, you don't know the story – "

"So tell me," Sam cut in.

Pike nodded. "Sure, sure. The fella who runs the gang is called Ramsey, Hank Ramsey, and he's just about the meanest hombre you ever saw, Sam. He makes ol' Delbert Hardy look sweet and gentle."

"That's hard to imagine. Go on."

"I admit it's a pretty bad bunch. I never should've throwed in with 'em. You know me, Sam. I'll cut some corners ever' now and then, but I ain't a real badman. Not like Ramsey and Trent and them others. I went along on a few of the jobs they pulled. They were too quick to shoot. They'd kill anybody who even looked like they might get in the way, whether they really did or not." Pike shook his head. "I couldn't abide those bloodthirsty ways. I just couldn't. So from then on I just did the cookin' and took care of the horses, a little blacksmithin' and such. I'm a decent cook and not a bad smith. Probably could've made a livin' at that if I'd wanted to."

"Too bad you didn't," Sam said.

"Yeah," Pike said. "Anyway, after a while it got to where I couldn't even stand to do that much, knowin' what sort of hombres they were, so I told Ramsey I was leavin'. Told him he didn't even have to give me my share of the loot if he'd just let me ride out. He said sure, for me to go ahead, no hard feelin's." The old-timer paused. "Then he tried to kill me. I barely got away with a whole hide."

"Why would Ramsey want to kill you?"

Pike held up two fingers. "Couple of reasons. I know where the gang's been hidin' all the loot from their robberies. Hank figured he couldn't afford to have me on the loose with knowledge like that in my head. The other reason is that he's loco, Sam. Once a member of the gang, always a member of the gang. Nobody rides away from Hank Ramsey. I've heard him say that more'n once."

"But you thought he would let you leave."

"I hoped he would. But I was ready for him to go back on his word, and he did. Ever since, they've been huntin' me. I remembered hearin' about you and this ranch, so I thought maybe if I could get here, you'd help me out, let me lie low here until things die down and Ramsey forgets about me. I remembered that, well, I hate to say it, but you sort of owe me . . ."

Sam nodded. There was no getting around the fact that Pike had saved his life back in Arkansas, even though the old-timer had been partly to blame for Delbert Hardy wanting to kill him. "Yes, I do. What happened this morning?"

"It started last night. Trent and another member of the gang, a fella name of Briscoe, jumped me. We traded shots, and I got ventilated. But I gave 'em the slip and then rode my horse to death tryin' to stay ahead of 'em until I got here. I figured I had to be close . . . hoped so, anyway . . . so I tried to make it on foot. Reckon I must've passed out, and that's when your boy found me. Say, he's a real humdinger, ain't he? Got plenty of sand, that boy."

"Yeah," Sam agreed. "Plenty of sand, but not much common sense sometimes." He looked at the old-timer and shook his head. "What am I going to do with you, Orion?"

Pike returned the look with one of innocence and hope. "What are you gonna do with me?" he repeated. "Why, considerin' all there is between us in the past, Sam, you're gonna help me. Ain't you?"

12

"You told him what?"

Sam saw the surprised, angry look on his wife's face and didn't blame her for feeling that way. "I told him he could stay here," he said again.

"An outlaw? A man who has an entire gang of other outlaws looking for him so they can kill him . . . and you invite him to stay?"

Sam had never believed in keeping things from Jenny. She was his partner in life and deserved the truth, he believed. But he wished there had been some way he could have shielded her from this. He didn't like being torn between his wife and the old friend who had saved his life.

"It's not like I asked Orion to move in permanently," he said. "He just needs a place to hole up for a while. Eventually Ramsey and the rest of that bunch will stop looking for him around here. Then he can move on."

"Do you really think they'll give up, Sam? From what you've told me, they seem pretty determined to kill him."

Sam and Jenny were alone in the kitchen. Tucker had gone back to the bunkhouse. As long as Sam was here, one of the hands didn't have to stay in the house.

He could look after Jenny and the kids.

"We'll keep Orion out of sight. Ramsey's men may lurk around these parts for a while, but when they don't catch even a glimpse of him, they'll figure he's moved on."

"I wouldn't think you'd like having those men sneaking around the ranch."

"I don't," Sam said. "I don't like it one little bit. But I'd just as soon not get in a shooting war with them, so it's better to let them decide on their own that Orion's given them the slip."

Jenny looked at him for a long moment and then sighed. "It seems like a risky plan," she said.

"It is," Sam agreed. "But I can't just throw Orion to the wolves, Jenny. I can't."

She put a hand on his arm and moved closer to him, slipping an arm around his waist and resting her head against his broad chest. "I know," she murmured. "Sam Blaylock is a man who's loyal to his friends. I don't suppose I'd have you any other way."

Sam breathed deep of the fragrance of her hair and enjoyed the warmth of his wife's body against him. He said quietly, "I don't know that Orion and I are actually friends anymore . . . but I owe him my life. There's no getting around that."

"But by helping him like this, *you'll* be saving *his* life, won't you?"

"Yeah. Between Titus bringing him in and you patching up his wounds and all of us letting him stay here . . . yeah, after this Orion Pike and I will be square, that's for sure."

\#

"What you reckon happened with Mr. Pike, back when Pa was a boy?" Titus asked his brother as he and Elijah worked in the corn field, pulling weeds from among the healthy plants.

"Why don't you ask Pa?" Elijah said.

That was the way Elijah was, Titus thought, always going for the simple, direct method, even when there was no chance it would work. In this case, not a hoot in hell.

"Pa won't talk about it," Titus said. "Not with us around, anyway."

"Then I suppose it's his business."

"Yeah, and it's something he's ashamed of, else he wouldn't mind us knowin' about it. I'll bet it's pretty bad."

"Pa?" Elijah sounded doubtful. "I don't think he ever did anything really bad. He's not that sort of man."

"Yeah, but Mr. Pike is. You've heard the way Ma's voice gets when she talks about him. She doesn't like him, and she doesn't want him here. And there's a reason somebody's always around, like they're standin' guard. That fella who got away must have partners, and they're still after Mr. Pike. Otherwise Pa wouldn't have told us to be on the lookout for strangers."

Almost three weeks had passed since the day Titus had found Orion Pike near the river and wound up in a shootout. During that time, Pike hadn't set foot outside the bunkhouse. Gabby even took his meals out to him. Pike was hiding from somebody, Titus was convinced of that. It was the only explanation that made any sense.

Also during that three weeks, Pike had grown stronger and begun to recover from the wounds he had suffered. The color was back in his face, and he could get up and move around without being too stiff about it now. Titus had found excuses to go out to the bunkhouse a few times and had spoken to Pike, but Gabby or Duane or Tucker would come along and run him off, like they were under orders to keep him from visiting with the man whose life he had saved.

That got under Titus's skin like a burr under a saddle.

So did the fact that his pa still wouldn't let him ride free over the ranch, even though the two weeks of punishment was over. Pa still insisted that Titus not leave the ranch headquarters unless one of the men was with him. The same was true for Elijah and Miriam. If that wasn't proof that Pa was still worried, Titus didn't know what it was.

He didn't particularly want to run into the sort of men who'd been after Pike before, but being confined chafed at him anyway. He had never liked being penned up, even when there was a good reason for it.

Today Gabby Darbins was sitting under a tree not far from the garden where Titus and Elijah labored. A rifle lay on the ground next to the old-timer, who was busy whittling on a piece of wood, concentrating so hard on what he was doing that his tongue stuck out one corner of his mouth. Titus straightened from his work, looked at Gabby for a minute, and said, "I'm gonna go get some water."

"We're almost done here," Elijah protested. "Another hour and we'll be finished."

"I'm thirsty now." Titus started for the edge of the garden.

Gabby saw him moving and called, "Where you goin', boy?"

"Back to the well for a drink!" Titus called. He waved vaguely toward the buildings, the nearest one of which was the barn about a hundred yards away.

Gabby hesitated, then nodded. "Go ahead," he said. "I can see you all the way from here."

Before Titus had gone fifty feet, though, Gabby was back at his whittling. Titus had figured that was what would happen.

As he circled the barn he didn't head for the well but for the bunkhouse instead. He knew that Tucker, Duane, and Randy were all at the sawmill this afternoon. His ma and Miriam were in the house, along with his pa. Titus knew he'd be in trouble if Pa caught him sneaking around the bunkhouse, but he figured the risk was worth it.

He ought to have the right to talk to Orion Pike. He had saved the fella's life, after all.

Titus went to the back door of the bunkhouse and eased it open. He stepped inside. The place was shadowy and quiet in the middle of the day like this. He started up the aisle between the row of bunks, looking for Pike.

A floorboard creaked behind him. Titus stopped and looked back over his shoulder . . .

Only to find himself staring down the barrel of a gun.

13

"Boy, what the hell are you doin'?" Orion Pike said as he lowered the revolver. "You know how close I come to blowin' a hole in you just now? In this bad light, you look as big as a man full-grown!"

Titus might have taken that as a compliment if he hadn't been shaken by having a gun pointed in his face. He swallowed and found his voice.

"I'm sorry, Mr. Pike. I didn't mean to scare you."

Pike scoffed. "Didn't scare me. I don't scare easy. Just bein' careful, that's all. Man who's got enemies can't afford to get too careless." He put the gun back in the holster on his hip. "Your pa send you to look for me?"

"No, sir. He don't know I'm here."

A smile appeared on Pike's weathered face. "Didn't figure as much, elsewise you wouldn't'a been slippin' in the back like that. Why'd you come sneakin' around?"

"I . . . I wanted to talk to you."

Pike looked a little surprised at that. "Really? What for?"

"Well . . . after that trouble we went through together a few weeks ago, I thought maybe it'd be a good thing if we got to know each other."

"You did, did you?" Pike sat down on the bunk he'd been using and waved a hand at one of the empty bunks. "Light and sit for a spell, then." A canny expression appeared on his face as Titus sat down. "I'll bet you want to know all about the mischief your pa got into, back when he was a youngster not much older than you."

"No, sir, I, uh, never even thought about that."

Pike let out a snort that showed how much he believed Titus's answer. "Knowin' some things about your pa that he don't want you to know might come in handy for a boy like you. But I never been the sort to tell tales on a fella, especially not one who's a friend. So you're outta luck there, sonny." A grin spread across Pike's face. "But if you want to hear some yarns about the things I've done and the places I've been, maybe play some cards while we're at it, might be I could oblige you."

Titus leaned forward eagerly. "I'd like that a lot, sir," he said.

"Don't bother sirrin' me. There's a deck of cards over yonder on that table where the hands play of an evenin'. Why don't you fetch 'em, and I'll show you a few things about poker. You can hear all about the life and times of Orion Pike while we're at it."

The minutes passed in a pleasant blur for Titus as he played cards with Pike and listened to the old-timer spin yarns about his colorful and exciting life. From the sound of it, Pike had been just about everywhere west of the Mississippi River, from the Rio Grande to the Canadian border, and everywhere he'd gone, some adventure had taken place. Titus was smart enough to know that some of the things Pike told him were exaggerated far beyond the reality of them, if not made up entirely, but he didn't care. He just liked listening to the old man talk.

After a while, though, he realized that he had been gone too long. Elijah and Gabby would be getting worried about him by now – or suspicious that he was up to something, which he was, of course – and it was late enough the men might come in from the sawmill without any warning.

"I've got to go," he said as he stood up.

"Don't want to get in trouble, eh?"

"It's not that." For some reason he didn't want Pike to think he was afraid. "I just have things to do, that's all."

"Well, I understand a man havin' things to do." A wistful note crept into Pike's voice. "But you'll come back to see me when you can, won't you? It gets mighty lonely out here in this bunkhouse by myself. I can sure use somebody to talk to."

He had the four ranch hands to talk to in the evenings, Titus thought, but he supposed the days got pretty long for Pike. He nodded and said, "Sure, I'll come back."

"Good. Next time I'll show you how to tell if a fella's bluffin' when you're playin' poker with him."

Titus could hardly wait.

#

Elijah and Gabby were on their way in from the garden when Titus met them. Even Elijah, who had a trusting soul, seemed a little suspicious of him, and Gabby definitely was. Titus deflected their questions about where he'd been by hinting that he'd been occupied in the outhouse for a while, and they didn't press the issue. Titus had a hunch they'd be watching him a little more closely from now on, though.

That didn't stop him from slipping away on several occasions during the next week and visiting Orion Pike in the bunkhouse. Titus thoroughly enjoyed those visits. Pike had been everywhere and done everything, and Titus drank it all in like a man dying of thirst who had stumbled onto a beautiful pool of cool, clear water.

Not only that, but the air of tension around Rancho Diablo had finally eased. Sam Blaylock and the ranch hands stopped standing guard over everyone all the time, although they were naturally alert for any signs of trouble, as always. That made it easier for Titus to spend time with Pike.

As they played poker in the bunkhouse one afternoon, Pike said, "Your pa ain't as nervous as he was for a while, is he?"

"Doesn't seem to be," Titus agreed.

"You know what that means . . . That fella you shot never came back lookin' for me."

"That's what I figure. You know, Orion, you never have told me why those hombres were gunnin' for you."

"No, I haven't, have I?" Pike frowned and rasped a thumbnail along his jaw. "Let's just say that them and me had ourselves a little disagreement."

"That's no answer and you know it," Titus said.

"Well, it's all the answer you're gettin', and while you were worryin' about that, I took this off the bottom of the deck right in front of you." Pike held up the ace of hearts. "You got to be able to talk and keep your eyes on the cards at the same time."

Titus grimaced. "Sorry, Orion. I appreciate all you're been teachin' me."

"Your ma probably wouldn't appreciate it if she knew you'd been spendin' so much time with me," Pike said with a chuckle. "She'd probably be afraid I was a heap bad influence on you."

Titus grinned. "She'd be right, wouldn't she?"

That brought a cackle of laughter from the old man. "Could be, boy, could be!"

A little later, Pike said, "I been thinkin' about that town down the river. Shooter's Cross, it's called?"

"That's right. On account of how back during the war against the Mexicans, a man called Shooter York set up little crosses to mark the distance and then climbed up on top of the peak they named after him later to shoot some of Santa Anna's soldiers."

Pike nodded. "Good-sized settlement, is it?"

"I reckon. There are a lot of houses and businesses, and more coming in all the time."

Pike rubbed his chin, turned his head a little, and

cut his eyes to the side. "Includin' some, uh, saloons?"

"Well, sure. There are half a dozen, maybe more." Titus felt ashamed as he added, "I've never been in any of 'em. Pa wouldn't stand for it."

"There's one thing I've learned over the years, boy . . . What a fella don't know ain't gonna hurt him. If you were to pay a visit to one o' those fine establishments and ol' Sam never found out, then there wouldn't be no harm done, would there?"

"You want me to go to a saloon?" Titus asked.

"Nope. I want you to take *me* to a saloon."

"But I thought . . . well, I thought you had to stay here. You know, in the bunkhouse. So if anybody's still looking for you, they can't find you."

Pike waved a gnarled hand. "Shoot, nobody's lookin' for me. If they were, they'd have given up and moved on by now. And I really need to get out and have me a mite of fun. I been stuck out here for dang near a month with no whiskey, nobody to play cards with you but you – no offense, son – and no, uh, how do I put this? No female companionship." Pike wiggled his bushy gray eyebrows.

Titus stared at him. "I figured you were too old for that!"

"Don't make me wallop you upside the head, son. Some things a man never gets too old for, and the soft touch of a woman is one of 'em. You'll be learnin' all about that 'fore too much longer, I expect. But be that as it may, Gabby told me they're all gonna be workin' at the sawmill tomorrow, gettin' a bunch of boards ready to load up, so that's our chance to slip away. Our chance to howl, boy! What do you say to that?"

"I don't know . . ." Titus said.

But even as he spoke, he knew better. This was an opportunity he couldn't pass up. And Pike was right, if they could make it to town and then get back without anybody knowing they were gone, what difference would it make? Where was the harm in that?

There wasn't any. So as Pike looked at him expectantly, Titus felt himself nodding and heard himself saying, "We'll give it a try . . . on one condition."

"What's that?"

"You tell me more about some of the trouble my pa got into when you knew him back in Arkansas."

A grin spread across Pike's face. "You got yourself a deal, boy. You got yourself a deal!"

14

Getting away from Rancho Diablo had been surprisingly easy. So easy, in fact, that Titus was starting to worry that it was all some sort of trick. His pa and Orion Pike were old friends, after all. Maybe they had set this up between them just to find out how far Titus would go to get into some mischief.

The answer was pretty far. Titus couldn't deny that. At least as far as Shooter's Cross, anyway.

The men were all at the sawmill this afternoon, which was pretty hot now that summer was about to arrive in Texas. Titus's mother and sister were in the house working on a quilt, and Elijah was somewhere with his nose stuck in a book, as usual. Titus didn't understand how anybody could read as much as his brother did. So many words had to be bad for the brain.

So it hadn't been any trouble to slip into the barn, saddle a couple of horses, and lead them into the woods. Then he'd headed for the bunkhouse to let Orion Pike know they were ready to go. The old man buckled on his gunbelt and grinned in anticipation as they made their way to the spot where Titus had left the horses. They mounted up and headed for Shooter's Cross.

As they neared the ferry, Titus gave in to his growing worry and said, "Maybe I should stay on this side of the river, Mr. Pike. You can go on into town, and then I'll meet you over here later when you're through."

Pike frowned and shook his head. "You can't do that. You'll miss out on all the fun. Besides, I need you with me. Anybody asks who I am, you're gonna introduce me as a new hand who's workin' on your pa's ranch. That's almost true, ain't it?"

Pike hadn't done anything approaching work while he was at Rancho Diablo, Titus thought, even though he was getting around pretty good now. Good enough to be going to town, anyway. But Titus didn't say anything about that. Instead, he asked, "Why do you need me to introduce you to folks? What does it matter that they who you are?"

"Sometimes people get a mite suspicious of strangers, especially lawmen. There's a lawman in this here Shooter's Cross, ain't there?"

"Yeah. Marshal Tolliver."

"Good lawman, is he?"

"I guess so. My pa seems to like him."

"If he's a good lawman, he's gonna keep up with the comin's and goin's in his town. He sees you with me, he'll figure I'm workin' for your pa and he won't be worried about me."

"You might be wrong about that," Titus said. "A lot of the people in town don't seem all that friendly toward us."

"Well, I still think it's a good idea. And you sure don't want to miss the fun, that's the main thing."

Now that the time was fast approaching, Titus was less and less sure about this. The idea of going into a saloon, of maybe even taking a drink and . . . and getting a good look at the gals who worked in those places, with their painted faces and spangled dresses . . . it sort of made his stomach do flip-flops. He wanted to experience those things, and at the same time he didn't. He'd never admit it to anybody, but he was scared.

The ferry came in sight, and Titus let out a little groan of dismay.

"What's wrong?" Pike asked.

"I didn't even think about the ferry. Pa knows the man who runs it. Next time he comes down here, Mr. Kendall's liable to tell him about takin' you and me across the river to the settlement."

Pike thought it over and nodded. "You don't have to worry about that, son," he told Titus. "Before that happens, I'll tell your pa about this myself. I'll tell him it was all my idea and that I made you come along with me."

The offer didn't strike Titus as being all that generous. What Pike had said was pretty much the truth, and Titus didn't see how it would keep him from getting into trouble.

"That ain't all," Pike went on. "I'll tell him you tried to stop me from leavin', and that the only reason you came after me is because you thought I wasn't strong enough to be ridin' around yet. You were just tryin' to take care of me, you see. Your pa can't be too mad at you for tryin' to look after his old friend, can he? The old friend who saved his life one time?"

Titus's eyes widened. "You saved my pa's life?"

"I sure did, and I'll tell you all about it when we get back." Pike licked his lips. "Right now I'm in need of a few shots of who-hit-John."

Titus couldn't pass up that offer. He told himself to put his worries behind him for now and just enjoy the experience.

When they reached the ferry, Eustace Kendall said, "Howdy, young Blaylock. How's your pa and the rest of your family?"

"Fine, Mr. Kendall," Titus answered. He thought he might as well get started spreading the story about Pike being a new ranch hand. "This is – "

"Jedidiah Finch," Pike said as he leaned down from the saddle to offer his hand to Eustace. "Pleased to make your acquaintance. I'll be ridin' for Rancho

Diablo."

Eustace shook hands with him. "Pleased to meet you as well, Mr. Finch. I'm Eustace Kendall. This here ferry is mine."

"And a fine-lookin' one it is. The boy and me will be goin' across the river in style."

Eustace grinned as he took down the poles on the side of the ferry. Titus and Pike dismounted and led their horses on board.

A few minutes later they led the horses onto the dock on the other side of the river. Pike paid Eustace for the trip. As they started along the street, Titus asked, "Why didn't you tell Mr. Kendall your right name?"

"'Cause he didn't have any reason to need it."

Titus supposed that was true, but he had a feeling there was some other reason behind the lie Pike had told. Habit, maybe.

Titus spotted Mitchell McCarthy standing near the ferry landing. He knew that his pa and the newspaperman didn't get along very well. Pa believed McCarthy had something to do with the outlaw Dick Dockett trying to rob him. Titus instinctively disliked McCarthy and wouldn't put it past him.

McCarthy frowned at them as they went past but didn't say anything, and Titus didn't meet the man's eye. Instead he looked along the street and told Pike, "The Wooden Owl Saloon is probably the biggest in town."

"What kind of a name is that?"

Titus smiled. "The place has got a big wooden owl hanging in front of it. According to Gabby, it was carved out of a tree stump. He helped the man who made it bring it to town."

"Now that I got to see," Pike said as he clapped a hand on Titus's back. "Lead on, son."

They walked along Main Street until they reached the Wooden Owl. Pike let out a whistle of admiration and amazement as he looked up at the carved bird that hung from the awning over the boardwalk in front of the saloon.

"You weren't joshin'," he said. "That's a big owl."

They stepped up onto the boardwalk, and Titus took a deep breath. The batwings were right there, ready to be pushed aside so he and Pike could go in. This was really going to happen. After today, Titus told himself, things might not ever be the same.

But before they could step into the saloon, a man emerged from the building, pushing through the batwings. He stopped short as he saw Titus and Pike standing there. His eyes widened in recognition, and his hand jerked toward the gun he carried butt-forward in a cross-draw rig at his waist.

15

That moment was frozen in Titus's mind, all the details etched sharply into place. He saw the man's florid face, the gray eyes above a prominent nose, the little broken veins in his cheeks, the sweeping, gray-streaked mustache, and the shelf-like jaw. He saw the flat-crowned black hat sitting squarely on the man's head, the dark suit, the string tie, the plaid vest and white shirt bulging out over the barrel chest and protruding gut.

Mostly, though, he saw the badge pinned to the lapel of the man's coat, and the shiny, nickel-plated surface of the gun as it came out of the holster.

The gun barely had a chance to clear leather, though, before Pike's Colt came crashing down on the man's head and knocked the black hat flying. The man fell to his knees on the boardwalk, and Pike kicked him in the face. The man dropped his gun and went over backward.

Pike paused just long enough to send the nickel-plated revolver spinning away down the boardwalk with another kick before he grabbed a stunned Titus's arm and practically threw him toward the horses.

"Mount up!" Pike ordered. "We got to get out of here!"

The whole business had happened in a couple of heartbeats. Pike had moved so fast Titus hadn't even seen him draw his gun. A little less than a month earlier, Pike had been at death's door. Today he was able to outdraw and buffalo some lawman Titus had never seen before.

"Come on, boy!" Pike said as he jammed his Colt back in its holster and yanked the reins loose from the hitch rack. "Let's go!"

Part of Titus knew that running away wasn't the right thing to do. This had to be some sort of misunderstanding.

But Pike had recognized the star packer, just as surely as the man had known him. And Pike admitted that he had sometimes been on the wrong side of the law in the past. Clearly he'd been afraid that the stranger would arrest him.

Titus didn't want that to happen. Pike was his friend now, and besides, his pa owed Pike a debt, even if Titus didn't know what it was all about.

Those thoughts flashed through Titus's brain in less than the blink of an eye. Then he lunged to the hitch rack, jerked his horse's reins loose, and leaped into the saddle.

Pike had already swung up. He banged his heels against his mount's flanks and sent the animal pounding along Main Street. Titus rode hard after him. Titus heard people shouting, saw from the corner of his eye as folks on the street pointed at him and Pike. The hope that they could slip in and out of Shooter's Cross without anybody paying much attention to them had vanished.

Now Titus just prayed they could get out of town without anybody shooting them.

With the horses galloping like that, it took only a moment to reach the river. The ferry was still at the dock. Eustace hadn't even put the poles up yet. Pike slowed his horse but didn't dismount. He rode out onto the dock and sent the animal leaping onto the ferry.

"Go!" he shouted at Eustace. "Get this thing movin'!"

Eustace just gaped at Pike in surprise and confusion. His mouth dropped open even wider when Pike drew his gun and pointed it at him.

"Now!"

By this time Titus had swung down and was leading his horse on board. "Better do what he says, Mr. Kendall," Titus told the old ferryman.

"Have you gone loco, young Blaylock?" Eustace demanded. "Your pa – "

Pike eared back the hammer of his revolver.

"I'm goin', I'm goin'!" Eustace said as he reached for the side poles.

"Leave 'em!" Pike ordered. "Just get us on the other side of the river! Boy, you help him!"

Titus didn't argue. He didn't think Pike would hurt him, but right now he didn't want to test that hunch.

Titus grabbed one of the spokes that stuck out from the capstan and started pushing against it while Eustace did the same. As the thick rope wrapped around the capstan tightened, the ferry practically shot out into the Brazos, at least compared to its usual leisurely pace. Titus glanced toward town. A crowd had gathered near the dock. People knew something was wrong, but most of them probably didn't know about the violent confrontation in front of the Wooden Owl Saloon. Those who had witnessed it would spread the story fast, though.

More commotion arose. Titus looked over his shoulder again and saw a burly, black-clad figure push through the crowd. Sunlight winked on the badge pinned to the man's coat. Titus's heart gave a hard thump as he realized that the lawman had a rifle in his hands.

People yelled in alarm and started to scatter as the man brought the rifle to his shoulder. The weapon boomed, but Titus barely heard it because his pulse was hammering so loud inside his skull. He flinched as the bullet smacked into the water near the ferry. The lawman would probably get the range with his second shot. Titus saw the man work the rifle's lever.

Then another man appeared beside the first and grabbed the rifle barrel, wrenching it skyward just as the lawman fired again. This shot didn't come anywhere near the ferry, which was more than halfway across the river now.

The lawman didn't fire again. Titus recognized the second man as Marshal Everett Tolliver, and it appeared that the two of them were jawing angrily at each other. Titus didn't know exactly what was going on, but he was glad he wasn't being shot at anymore, at least for the moment.

A minute later the ferry grounded next to the dock on the far side of the river. Pike was still in his saddle. He hadn't dismounted. He rode off the ferry hurriedly.

"Come on, boy," he urged. "We got to get back to the ranch."

"I'm sorry, Mr. Kendall," Titus told the ferryman. "I hope you're all right."

"I'm fine," Eustace called after them as Titus urged his horse after Pike's, "but I got a hunch you may not be, young Blaylock!"

Titus heard that and knew Eustace was right. Pa was going to be mighty upset about this.

"Mr. Pike, who was that man?" Titus asked as they rode away from the river. "Why'd you hit him?"

"Damn lawdog," Pike bit off. "Deputy U.S. Marshal name of Herrick, Josiah Herrick. He's been chasin' after me and the fellas I used to ride with for a long time now. Mean son of a buck, Herrick is. One of those lawmen who uses his badge as an excuse to ride roughshod over anybody he don't like. He'll kill a man just as quick as look at him and then claim it was all in the line o' duty, but that ain't always true. Herrick, he just likes to kill!"

Titus could believe that. He had seen the way the man grabbed a rifle and started shooting at them as they crossed the river.

"He's nearly clapped me in irons a few times before

now," Pike went on, "and he don't like it that I've always managed to slip away from him, like today. That's why I didn't give him a chance when I recognized him. I knew he'd blow a hole in my belly and claim I was resistin' arrest. Probably would've gunned you down, too, and tell ever'body you tried to help me."

"How does somebody that brutal get to be a lawman?"

"Oh, you don't know the half of it, son. Most of those badge-toters are worse'n the so-called outlaws they're chasin'."

Titus had his doubts about that, but he didn't argue. Right now he just wanted to get back to Rancho Diablo. No matter how mad Pa got when he heard about this – and he'd get mighty mad, that was certain – Titus knew he could count on his father to handle things. No matter what the problem was, Sam Blaylock could straighten it out. Titus had every confidence in the world in him.

"This Marshal Herrick is liable to follow us," Titus called to Pike over the sound of their running horses.

"I know he will! He's like a blasted ol' bloodhound once he gets the scent. But I'm countin' on your pa to stop him."

It looked like Titus wasn't the only one who had a lot of confidence in Sam Blaylock. But would his pa take a stand against the law like that, even though the lawman was a bloodthirsty killer? Titus couldn't help but wonder about that.

They were about to find out, because there was Rancho Diablo, right in front of them.

16

Sam had come back to the house from the sawmill a few minutes earlier. He had the window in the office wide open, hoping to get a breath of air on this hot day, so he heard the pounding hoofbeats well before the riders reached the house. By the time they did, he was on the front porch with a Henry rifle in his hands, because nobody would be headed for Rancho Diablo that fast on a day like this unless there was trouble.

Sam's jaw clenched and his hands tightened on the rifle as he recognized Titus and Orion Pike. What the devil was Pike doing out of the bunkhouse?

Jenny came onto the porch behind Sam. "Titus!" she exclaimed when she saw the two riders reining in. "What are you doing?" She echoed Sam's thought. "Mr. Pike, you're supposed to be in the bunkhouse!"

Titus opened his mouth to answer, but Pike spoke up first. "We got trouble, Sam, bad trouble. The law's on our trail."

"On *your* trail, maybe," Sam snapped. "What happened?"

"The boy and me, we went into that town downriver . . . I was just lookin' for a little entertainment, you understand, I been stuck in that bunkhouse a long time . . . but no sooner did we get there than who do we run into? A blasted U.S. marshal who's been lookin' for me!"

"Good Lord! You didn't kill him, did you?"

Pike snorted. "Of course not! I just got my gun out first and walloped him over the head so he couldn't kill me! Then me and the boy lit a shuck outta there."

"A lot of people saw me, Pa," Titus said. "And Mr. Kendall carried us back and forth across the river. Somebody's bound to tell that marshal where to look for us."

Sam's brain was spinning, and his guts almost felt like the earth had dropped out from underneath him. He had risked a lot, up to and including his family's lives, to help Orion Pike, and this was the way the old scoundrel had paid him back, by sneaking off to town and getting Titus in trouble with the law.

Pike was saying, "I thought maybe you could let me hide out again – "

"No," Sam cut in. His voice was flat and hard. "Not this time. Not here."

"But, Sam . . ." A whining tone crept into Pike's voice. "That marshal, he'll shoot me on sight. He's got a powerful hate for me."

"It's true, Pa," Titus put in. "The marshal reached for his gun as soon as he saw Mr. Pike."

Sam shook his head. "There are hiding places up in the hills, Orion. You're on your own. Take that horse you're on and get out of here. That's all I can do for you."

"That don't sound like you, Sam," Pike said as he scowled. "You ain't never been the sort of man to turn your back on an old friend, a friend who – "

"Stop right there. Don't you throw that in my face again. Not after what you've done." Sam took a deep breath. "I'll do what I can to help you, but not here. Head for the hills, Orion. That's your best chance."

Pike stared at him for a moment, then abruptly lifted the reins and jerked the horse around. He banged his heels on its flanks and sent it galloping away from the house.

With a stricken look, Titus watched the old man go. He turned his gaze toward Sam and said, "Pa, you can't just run him off like that. You didn't see that marshal. He's a killer. He's worse than any outlaw – "

"I'm sure that's what Orion told you," Sam said. His voice was harsh as he went on, "But maybe you don't know as much as you think you do, boy. Now put your horse up and get in the house."

"Pa – "

"Do what I told you, Titus. *Now.*"

Jenny laid a hand on Sam's arm. He glanced over at her, saw that she was angry, too, but she had signs of maternal sympathy on her face.

"I know what I'm doing," he told her. Elijah and Miriam had come out onto the porch, too. "All of you get inside. That lawman probably isn't far behind them."

"Be careful, Sam. If that man is as bad as Titus and Mr. Pike said – "

"It'll be all right," Sam said. "Just go on in."

Jenny nodded and turned to usher her other two children into the house. No sooner were they gone than Sam heard hoofbeats. He tensed for a second before he realized they were coming from the direction of the sawmill, not the road that led downriver.

Four riders came into view: Tucker, Duane, Gabby, and Randy. Their mounts were moving at a fast trot. As they came up to the ranch house and reined in, dust from the horses' hooves swirled in the hot air.

Tucker dismounted quickly and came up onto the porch. "We heard horses, and then that fella Pike galloped past the mill. What's going on, Sam?"

"Trouble. Pike and Titus rode down to Shooter's Cross and ran right into a U.S. marshal who's been on Orion's trail."

"Saints above!" Duane said. "How did they get away?"

"Pike pistol-whipped the lawman."

Gabby shook his head. "Oh, Lordy, that ain't good. I

thought that old troublemaker was still lyin' low, in case those varmints who were after him are still around here, consarn it."

"That was the plan," Sam agreed. "Pike thought differently and talked Titus into helping him."

"What happens now?" Tucker asked, getting right down to business as was his nature.

"I expect we'll be getting a visit from the law pretty soon. You boys will follow my lead?"

"You don't even have to ask, Mr. Blaylock," Randy said.

Titus emerged from the barn and hurried toward the house. Sam didn't say anything, just jerked a thumb at the front door. Head down, with a contrite expression, Titus went past the men and into the house.

He hadn't been out of sight more than thirty seconds when Sam heard more hoofbeats, this time coming from the road to Shooter's Cross. His prediction was about to come true.

Duane, Gabby, and Randy dismounted and joined Sam and Tucker on the porch. All of them were armed. Duane carried an ivory-handed Colt .44 in a hand-tooled holster because he liked fancy things, but the gun was perfectly serviceable and he was good with it. Gabby had the ten-gauge Greener he favored. Randy carried a Henry rifle. Counting Sam's handgun and rifle and Tucker's three Tranters, the five of them made a mighty formidable bunch.

The two men who rode up to the house a few minutes later had the law on their side, though. Sam had never seen the man with Marshal Everett Tolliver before, but he had a badge pinned to his coat and Sam had no doubt he was the U.S. marshal Pike and Titus had mentioned.

"Hello, Everett," Sam said as the two lawmen reined to a halt in front of the porch. "I won't insult you by asking what brings you out here."

Tolliver leaned forward slightly in the saddle to ease his muscles. He wasn't a man who did a lot of riding, since his job kept him in town most of the time.

"It appears that you've been harboring a fugitive, Sam. If you turn him over to us, there won't be any trouble."

"As far as I know, I'm not harboring anybody, fugitive or otherwise," Sam replied. "Who's that with you?"

Before Tolliver could say anything, the red-faced man said, "I'm Deputy United States Marshal Josiah Herrick, and you're under arrest!"

"Ease up a little, Marshal," Tolliver advised. "That's not the way to go about this."

Sam's back had stiffened already. This Marshal Herrick might not be as bad as Pike made him out to be, but he definitely rubbed Sam the wrong way.

"Under arrest for what?"

"Like Marshal Tolliver said, harboring a fugitive. Accessory after the fact to robbery and murder. Conspiracy." Herrick swept the men on the porch with a baleful glare. "You're all under arrest! Drop those guns right now, or by God I'll see you all hanged!"

17

It was one of those moments when a lot hung in the balance. Men's lives, for sure.

But more than that was at stake. Given the fact that they outnumbered the lawmen by more than two to one, Sam was confident he and his men could blast Tolliver and Herrick out of their saddles. Some of them might taste lead, too, but the lawmen would wind up dead on the ground.

If that happened, the survivors of the shootout would be murderers in the eyes of society. They would be on the run from the law for the rest of their days. And this life Sam had just started to build for his family here on Rancho Diablo . . . well, it would be shot all to hell, too.

All it would take to start that explosion of destructive violence was a single shot.

Instead, Everett Tolliver said, "Damn it, I told you to ease off, Herrick!" He moved his horse so that he was between the federal star packer and the men on the porch. "You, too, Sam! Everybody take a deep breath and settle down. Nobody's under arrest."

Herrick blustered, "You can't do that. You have no jurisdiction."

"You tried to kill a boy while you were in my town," Tolliver told him. "That gives me the jurisdiction to arrest *you*."

"I was trying to apprehend a fugitive!"

"Titus Blaylock isn't wanted for anything."

"He was aiding and abetting that outlaw in his escape."

"There haven't been any charges filed against him," Tolliver said. "In the eyes of the law, he was just an innocent bystander, and so was Eustace Kendall. But you put both of their lives at risk by taking a shot at that ferry. The way I see it, I can lock you up for that, and I will unless you calm down."

Herrick's face was so red he looked like he was about to pop a blood vessel, but after a moment he gave Tolliver a curt nod. "All right, Marshal," he said. "Exactly what is it you want?"

Tolliver looked over at Sam. "The whole story," he said. "And I want it now, or else I might just ride away and let you stubborn fools kill each other."

Sam decided it was time to tell the truth, or part of it, anyway. "Remember that dead outlaw I brought into town about a month ago? Jonah Trent?"

"Trent!" Herrick burst out. "You say he's dead? He was part of Hank Ramsey's gang, too!"

Caustically, Tolliver said, "I could have told you about Trent, Marshal, if you had checked in with me when you rode into town like you should have, instead of choosing to search for the men you're after on your own."

"I'm a federal lawman," Herrick said with a haughty scowl. "My authority supersedes that of a local marshal."

"There's such a thing as professional courtesy," Tolliver snapped. "Go on, Sam."

"I didn't actually find Trent's body," Sam said. "My boy Titus showed me where it was. You see, Titus was out gallivanting around when he found a wounded man upriver from here. He was trying to help the man when two more hombres jumped them and tried to kill them. Orion Pike, the one who was wounded, killed Trent."

Sam left out the part about Miriam being involved. It didn't really matter, he thought, and not mentioning his daughter would spare her some potential embarrassment.

Tolliver looked over at Herrick. "This man Pike is the one you're after?"

"He's a member of Hank Ramsey's gang," Herrick said. "I'm after all of them. They've stolen mail pouches from trains in several of their robberies. That makes them federal criminals."

"Pike's not riding with Ramsey's gang anymore," Sam said.

Herrick let out a contemptuous snort. "Is that what he told you?"

"It makes sense. If Pike was still one of them, why did Trent and the other man try to kill him?"

Herrick had no answer for that. Tolliver asked, "What happened to the other man who was with Trent?"

"He was wounded and lit out." Sam didn't explain that Titus had fired the shot that wounded the outlaw. "That's the last we've seen of him or any of Ramsey's other men. They haven't been around here."

"Except for Pike," Herrick said. "You've been harboring him."

"He was wounded. We took care of him. That's what folks do."

"People who are the next thing to outlaws themselves," Herrick said. "Marshal Tolliver has told me about you, Blaylock. You have a bad reputation."

"That's not what I said," Tolliver protested.

Tucker spoke up, saying quietly, "You ought to ask the army what sort of reputation Sam Blaylock has, mister. He's one of the best scouts who ever rode with the cavalry."

"And a better man you won't find anywhere under heaven," Duane added.

Herrick sneered. "So your friends speak up for you,

Blaylock. I'm not surprised. They're probably as crooked as you are."

Tucker and Duane tensed. Sam held out a hand and motioned for them to rein in their anger at the federal lawman's insult.

Tolliver said, "Sam, did you know this man Pike was an outlaw?"

"I knew he had a checkered past," Sam replied honestly. "I used to know him when I was a boy back in Arkansas. But I swear to you, Everett, I never saw him commit a crime, and he told me he wasn't part of Ramsey's bunch anymore. The fact that they were after him makes me believe he was telling me the truth. Sure, I let him stay here while he healed up. I didn't have personal knowledge of any charges against him."

"Good Lord!" Herrick said. "He admitted he used to ride with Ramsey! You should have known he was wanted."

Sam shrugged. "For all I knew, if he ever had any charges against him, they could have been dropped."

"Sam . . ." Tolliver's voice had a slightly chiding tone. "You're one of the smartest men I know. You should have been able to figure it out."

"Everybody's dumb sometimes," Sam said. That was sure the truth, he thought. He should have sent Pike away as soon as the man was able to travel.

"Did your boy Titus know what sort of man Pike is?"

Sam shook his head. "All Titus knew was that Pike was an old friend of mine, and he didn't even know that the day he found him. They became friends, too. Titus meant no harm by going into town with him today."

"A likely story," Herrick said with another disgusted snort.

"It's the truth."

"We may need to talk to Titus sometime," Tolliver said, "but right now it seems to me he's in the clear." He gave Herrick a hard look. "But that leaves Pike. Where is he, Sam?"

"I don't know." The next words out of Sam's mouth

were the first actual lie he had told during this confrontation. "Titus came back to Rancho Diablo alone. I guess Pike took off for the tall and uncut."

The other four men on the porch regarded the pair of lawmen stoically. If Sam Blaylock said it, it was good enough for them.

Herrick lifted his reins and started to turn his horse away. "I'm going to search all these buildings," he said.

Sam moved the barrel of his Henry so that it pointed at Herrick. "I wouldn't do that, mister!" he said. "You're on my land, and *I* haven't seen anything proving you're a U.S. marshal. For all I know, you're just a trespasser – and I've got a right to shoot trespassers."

"Sam . . ." Tolliver said.

"I mean it, Everett. This so-called marshal's got no proof the man he's after is here, and I won't have him stomping around my house or any of my property, for that matter, and disturbing my family. I want him off Rancho Diablo right now."

Trembling with fury, Herrick said, "Tolliver, do something about this!"

"Like you pointed out, Marshal, your authority supersedes mine. In fact, my jurisdiction runs out at the edge of town."

"By God, I'll charge *you* with obstruction of justice, too!"

"Come to think of it," Tolliver grated out, "I haven't seen any real proof you're who you say you are. Anybody can pin a badge to his coat. If it ever came down to a trial, I might have to testify on behalf of Mr. Blaylock here and say that he was just defending his property when he did . . . whatever it is he does."

"You heard the man, Herrick," Sam said. "Get off my ranch, and stay off. We all know you now, and we won't take kindly to you coming back."

Herrick shook a finger at Sam and the other men on the porch. "I will see you hanged, or behind bars at the very least! You, too, Tolliver! You're a disgrace to the badge you wear!"

"I think you better git," Tolliver said.

Still looking like he was going to explode at any second, Herrick wheeled his horse and cruelly jabbed his heels into its flanks. He rode out, taking the trail that led to the ferry and Shooter's Cross.

Tolliver looked at Sam and sighed. "You put me in a mighty bad position here. Herrick can't hang either of us for obstruction, but he can make our lives miserable."

"I know that, Everett, and I'm truly sorry."

"I'll follow Herrick and make sure he goes back to town. But he's liable to be back here, and when he comes, he'll bring a whole posse of marshals with him. If there's anything you can do to fix this, Sam, you'd better do it."

"Don't worry," Sam said. "I intend to."

18

As soon as Everett Tolliver had ridden off after Herrick, Sam turned to Tucker and said, "Go after them, but keep your distance. I just want to know for sure that they go back to town."

Tucker nodded. He headed for the barn to saddle a horse.

"What do you want us to do, Sam?" Duane asked.

"The three of you can go on back to the sawmill and finish loading that lumber. We'll need to take it to town in the morning."

As Duane, Gabby, and Randy departed, Sam went into the house. Jenny was waiting for him.

"I don't care if that man did save your life, Sam Blaylock," she said without giving him a chance to speak. "I want him off this ranch."

A weary smile creased Sam's face as he hung the Henry on a couple of pegs near the door. "No more than I do. That's twice now Orion Pike's nearly gotten my son shot. That's enough."

"More than enough, if you ask me." Jenny paused. "What are you going to do?"

"Go find him, I suppose. Tell him to move on. If he's

well enough to go to town, he's well enough to leave this part of the country." Sam shrugged. "He could probably do with some supplies to keep him going for a few days."

Jenny's angry expression softened just a little. "I can put together a bag of provisions," she said. "That won't hurt anything, and if it'll help get him away from our home . . ."

"That's a good idea," Sam agreed. "I want to have a talk with Titus while you're doing that. Where is he?"

"In his room. I sent all the children upstairs when I thought that . . ."

She didn't have to go on. Sam knew what she meant. She'd been trying to get the kids out of the line of fire in case any shooting broke out.

Jenny headed for the kitchen while Sam went upstairs to the room Titus shared with Elijah. He opened the door without knocking.

Elijah sat on the bed looking worried.

There was no sign of Titus.

"Where's your brother?" Sam asked.

Elijah shook his head. "I don't know. He said he had something to do. I thought he meant the outhouse, but he hasn't come back yet."

Anger welled up inside Sam, but he tamped it down. To be fair, he had told Titus to get in the house, but he hadn't told him to stay there.

He said, "I'll find him," and started to turn away.

Elijah got up hurriedly and slipped past Sam. "Let me," he said over his shoulder. "I'll bring him to your office."

Sam started to tell the boy to come back, then changed his mind and said, "All right." He supposed Elijah wanted to warn his brother about how much trouble he was in. Elijah was a good-natured sort and always worried about Titus no matter how often Titus tried to take advantage of him.

Sam went to his office and sat down to wait. Worries gnawed at his thoughts. He figured Shooter's Cross was buzzing by now about what had happened, and when

Tolliver and Herrick got back to town, it was inevitable that word would get around quickly about how Sam Blaylock had been sheltering a notorious outlaw at his ranch. That was how Mitchell McCarthy would make it sound, anyway. Sam could see the headline in the newspaper now: RANCHO DIABLO REFUGE FOR LAWBREAKERS!

McCarthy would play it up big and lay it on thick, all right, until the few people in the settlement who had been willing to give Sam the benefit of the doubt before would be forced to conclude that he was little better than an outlaw himself. If the entire community turned on him, it would be that much more difficult to make a success out of Rancho Diablo.

Sam sat at his desk brooding about that until a footstep at the door made him look up. Elijah stood there looking even more worried that he had been earlier.

"Titus isn't in the outhouse," Elijah reported. "He's not in the barn or the bunkhouse, either. I can't find him anywhere, Pa!"

Sam got to his feet. "He has to be around."

Elijah shook his head and said, "I've looked. I . . . well, I know all his hiding places, Pa, the places he goes when he's trying to get out of doing his chores. He's not in any of them."

"Then he's here in the house."

"I don't think so."

"Then where – " Sam stopped short as another possibility occurred to him. "Oh, no. He wouldn't. Not after all the trouble he's already got himself into."

"I don't know, Pa. When Titus thinks he's right, he can be mighty stubborn."

"Come on. Let's take another look around. Don't say anything to your mother or your sister just yet, though," Sam added. "I don't want them worrying and then have him turn up."

But what he really wanted was for Titus to turn up, he realized. A cold ball of fear sat in his belly when he thought about where Titus might have gone. It just seemed loco that the boy would have taken off after Orion Pike, but in all honesty, Sam couldn't rule it out.

Fifteen minutes later, he was forced to conclude that it was more than possible. It was likely. Because as Elijah had said, Titus was nowhere around the ranch headquarters. The horse he had ridden to Shooter's Cross was in the barn.

But the animal was unsaddled, and in his search of the barn, Sam hadn't seen Titus's saddle, either. That meant the boy could have transferred it to another mount.

Sam was going to have to tell Jenny. He couldn't keep Titus's disappearance from her.

"Elijah, saddle up your pony and ride to the sawmill," Sam said. "Tell Duane, Randy, and Gabby I said for them to get back here as fast as they can."

"Are you going to look for Titus?" Elijah asked.

"I reckon I'd better."

"He went after Mr. Pike, didn't he?"

"That's the way it looks to me. Now get along and do what I told you!"

"Yes, sir!"

Sam walked heavily toward the house. He wasn't looking forward to telling Jenny that one of her sons was missing.

When he came into the kitchen, she pointed to a burlap bag sitting on the table and said, "I've got those supplies ready for – " She stopped, and her eyes widened in alarm as she saw his face. "Sam, what is it? What's wrong?"

"Titus is nowhere around," he said. "I reckon he must've gone after Orion."

Jenny's hand went to her mouth. "Oh, Sam, no!"

"Now, don't worry," he said, trying to sound reassuring. "I was going to look for Orion to start with, remember? Now I'll just be looking for Titus, too. And when I send Orion packing, I'll bring Titus back with me."

She clutched at his arm. "But . . . but what if he and Pike have already left the ranch? What if Titus has run away for good?"

"He wouldn't do that," Sam said, "and even if he's got some fool idea like that in his head, he hasn't had time to get very far. I'll take the boys with me, and we'll run him down without any trouble. You wait and see."

Jenny shook her head. "I'm coming with you."

"No, you're not. Somebody has to stay here and look after Elijah and Miriam. Shoot, if Miriam finds out that Titus has run off, *she's* liable to want to go look for him, too!"

Anger flashed in Jenny's eyes. "Don't make fun of me, Sam. Not now."

"I'm not," he told her. "At least I didn't mean to. I'm just saying that we'll bring Titus back here safe and sound. I'm sure of it."

"You'd better."

He leaned over and brushed his lips across his wife's forehead. "It's a promise."

Sam hoped it was one he could keep.

19

By the time Sam got his horse saddled, Elijah was back from the sawmill with Duane, Gabby, and Randy. Also, Tucker had returned from watching Tolliver and Herrick cross the Brazos on Eustace Kendall's ferry and go back to Shooter's Cross.

"What's wrong, boss?" Gabby asked. "The young'un said you wanted us to rattle our hocks back here."

"Titus is gone," Sam told the men. "My hunch is that he's headed to the hills to look for Orion Pike. I'm not sure why – out of some misguided sense of friendship, I imagine – but the important thing is that we're going to find them and bring Titus back.""What about Pike?" Tucker asked.

"Send him on his way," Sam said. "He's no longer welcome on Rancho Diablo."

Tucker nodded.

Sam slung the bag of supplies on his saddle and tied it down. He mounted up and turned his horse toward the wooded hills that rolled away from the Brazos to the west. There were plenty of hiding places in those thickets. Finding Pike might not be as easy as he'd made it sound.

But Tucker was very skilled at following a trail, Duane wasn't bad, and Sam was pretty good at reading sign himself.

"This is the way Pike was going when he rode out," Sam said to his companions. "We'll follow his trail for long as we can. If we lose it, we'll split up and try to find it again."

A few minutes later, Tucker pointed out some fresh tracks that ran alongside the ones they had been following. "Looks like Titus caught up to him here, Sam," he said. "I recognize those prints those horseshoes left. They belong to that brown mare with the blaze face and the one white stocking."

Sam nodded. He knew the horse Tucker was talking about. Thinking back, he didn't remember seeing it in the barn when he'd been out there looking for Titus.

"That's him, all right," he said. "At least we know they're together and that we're on the right trail."

Once the tracks veered away from the river, they were more difficult to see, but there were other indications that the two riders had passed this way. Broken branches, crushed grass, recently overturned rocks . . . all those little signs were like a map to the eyes of a man like Tucker.

The terrain rose steadily and became more rugged. This was still Rancho Diablo range, but Sam hadn't had a chance to explore it thoroughly. The landscape was honeycombed with brush-choked gullies, rocky ridges, and narrow creeks with shallow but steep banks. The trail they were following twisted back and forth to avoid those natural obstacles.

"Could be anything hidin' in this wilderness," Gabby muttered. "Wouldn't surprise me none if we run into a bunch of Comanch' or a grizzly bear."

"Don't let your imagination run away with you," Sam said. "The Comanches are a long way northwest of here unless they're on another of those big raids, and we'd have heard about that. And this isn't bear country."

"How about panthers?" Duane asked. "Any panthers

around here?"

"Well, there could be, but I reckon they'd hear us coming and be more scared of us than we are of them. We have to worry more about humans than – "

A sudden rattle of gunfire in the distance interrupted Sam. He reined in and sat up straight in the saddle as bleak lines etched themselves in his face. The other men brought their horses to a stop as well. After a moment the shots trailed off and then stopped.

"That don't sound too good," Gabby said.

Sam looked over at Tucker. "You're sure Marshal Herrick went back to Shooter's Cross?"

"Of course I'm sure," Tucker said. "I saw him with my own eyes."

"Sorry," Sam said. "I knew better than to ask. Anyway, Herrick's even less familiar with the country around here than we are. There's no way he could have gotten ahead of us and ambushed Pike."

"Maybe those shots don't have anything to do with Pike and Titus," Duane suggested. "Could be somebody out hunting."

From the sound of Duane's voice it was clear he didn't really believe that, and none of the other men looked like they did, either.

"We'd better go find out," Sam said. He hitched his horse into motion. The other men followed. They weren't worried about following the trail now. Instead they just rode quickly in the direction of the gunshots they'd heard.

It was difficult to judge the distance of such things by sound. Sam figured the shots had come from somewhere between a mile and two miles away. When he estimated that they had gone about a mile, he slowed his horse and held up a hand.

"We don't want to ride right into trouble," he said quietly.

They went forward now at a slower and more careful pace. Sam had been listening intently for more shots or any other noises that were out of place in this sparsely populated landscape, but he hadn't heard anything.

He smelled something, though, as a faint scent of woodsmoke drifted to his nostrils. He signaled sharply for the others to halt again. The smell of smoke got a little stronger. Somewhere up ahead, within a few hundred yards, somebody had built a fire.

Using hand signals, Sam told the men to dismount. He had worked with Tucker and Duane in dangerous situations like this, so he knew he could count on them. Gabby and Randy were more unknown quantities. Neither of them were short on courage or loyalty, but Sam didn't know how they would handle themselves if it came down to a fight.

He had to trust them, though, at least until he knew exactly what sort of odds they were facing. *Somebody* besides Pike and Titus was out here. From the sound of the shots earlier, several men had been involved.

One name loomed in Sam's mind: Hank Ramsey. He had been convinced that the outlaw leader had moved on to look for Pike elsewhere, but there was no proof of that. Maybe Ramsey had known all along that Pike was at Rancho Diablo but had been playing it cagy. He might not have wanted to launch an all-out attack on the ranch, an attack that could have cost him the lives of a number of his men. Ramsey might be smart enough to just lie low and wait for Pike to leave the safety of the bunkhouse. In that case, Titus and Pike could have ridden right into some bad trouble.

Only one way to find out, Sam told himself. He motioned for the men to tie their horses to trees and then follow him.

They stole through the forest as quietly as possible, following the scent of woodsmoke. After a few minutes, Sam heard voices ahead of them. He stopped and listened, trying to pinpoint them. When he had a pretty good idea where the men were, he crooked a finger at Tucker and gestured for the other three to wait where they were.

Sam and Tucker took off their hats, then bellied

down and crawled through a thick stand of brush that extended for more than fifty yards. They had to take it slow and easy because the ground was carpeted with years worth of fallen leaves. Luckily, rot had set in, which kept the leaves from crackling too much. Any sounds they made were too faint to be heard more than a few feet away.

Finally they came to the edge of the thicket and stopped where they could peer through gaps in the branches without revealing their presence. Ahead of them, open ground sloped gently upward for about a hundred feet before reaching the much steeper slope of an upthrust bluff. Several crude lean-tos had been erected out of brush and tree branches against the bluff, and in front of them was a stone-enclosed fire pit. The ashes in the pit told Sam this camp had been here for quite a while. Probably close to a month, he thought, because that was when Hank Ramsey's gang had discovered that Orion Pike was at Rancho Diablo.

Habit made Sam do a quick head count. He saw seven men. A couple of them knelt beside the fire to get it going again. Two more men were unsaddling some horses in a rope corral strung between some trees. Sam counted the horses as well and came up with nine, including the blaze-faced mare that Titus had taken from the barn.

One man stood on each side of the camp, holding rifles and obviously standing guard. They were all the same sort as the late Jonah Trent . . . hard-faced, hard-bitten hombres who were well-acquainted with the dim and lonely trails.

That left one man, and he stood in front of one of the lean-tos. Sam couldn't see him very well because the man's back was partially toward him. Sam could tell that he had a black spade beard and was tall and wiry. He carried himself with a casual arrogance. Sam had a hunch he was looking at Hank Ramsey.

"You might as well give it up, Orion," the man said. "You know you're going to tell me what I want to know sooner or later."

From the shadows of the lean-to, a strained voice said, "Why don't you just . . . go to hell, Hank?"

That confirmed Sam's hunch about the man with the spade beard, and also his theory about Ramsey lying low and waiting for the right moment to make his move against Pike. That moment had come today at last.

But where *was* Titus? That question hammered inside Sam's brain. The horse was here. Titus had to be, too.

Unless he was lying dead somewhere in the woods.

"I don't care what you . . . do to me," Pike went on from inside the lean-to. Sam could barely make him out now. Pike sat at the back of the crude structure, propped up against the bluff that formed its rear wall. "I ain't gonna . . . talk."

"You always were a stubborn old buzzard," Ramsey said. "But we'll see how stubborn you are once Holcomb starts working on the boy. You know how Holcomb is with that knife of his."

Cold fear and hot rage filled Sam at those callous, cruel words, mingled with relief at the knowledge that Titus was still alive. His muscles tensed, and Tucker must have noticed that because the younger man touched Sam's shoulder. Sam forced himself to calm down and gave Tucker a nod. Charging into the outlaw camp with no plan would likely just get Titus killed, not to mention himself and his friends.

But where was Titus? That question was answered when Pike didn't say anything in response to Ramsey's threat. The outlaw leader turned and motioned to one of the men beside the fire. The man went over to one of the other lean-tos and reached in to drag Titus into the open. The boy's arms were tied behind him and he looked shaken, but other than that he appeared to be all right. His captor shoved him toward the lean-to where Pike and Ramsey were. Titus stumbled but managed to stay on his feet.

Ramsey's hand shot out and grabbed Titus by the

throat, jerking him closer. "All right, Pike," Ramsey said. "Either tell me where you hid that money you stole from us, or I'll tell Holcomb to start carving this boy into little pieces."

20

A part of Sam's brain was still working coherently enough to tell him that Pike had lied to him. Ramsey's words were enough to prove that. Pike hadn't just run out of the gang, and Ramsey wasn't after him because of pride or because Pike knew where all their loot was cached.

No, Pike had double-crossed them and stolen some of that loot for himself when he ran out on the gang, Sam knew now. And somehow, that knowledge didn't surprise him.

But it didn't really matter, either. Pike's actions were unimportant except for the way they impacted Titus's safety at this moment.

Tucker's hand tightened on Sam's shoulder again. Sam looked over at his friend and saw Tucker motion behind them with his head. He knew what Tucker meant. As slowly and quietly as they had approached the outlaw camp, they began backing away from it.

Leaving was one of the hardest things Sam had ever done. He listened for the screams of pain as the owlhoot called Holcomb began torturing Titus. Instead he just heard the low murmur of men continuing to talk. Maybe

Pike was spilling his guts, or maybe the old man was still trying to stall. Sam didn't know, but he knew there was no time to waste.

When they reached the far side of the thicket that ringed the camp, Sam and Tucker rolled to their feet. Sam grabbed Tucker's arm and whispered, "We've got to get in there!"

Tucker nodded. "I reckon we can work our way around to the top of that bluff above the camp."

Instantly, Sam saw what Tucker meant. He said, "Then we can slide down it and take them by surprise while Duane, Gabby, and Randy are hitting them from the front."

"Yeah. You grab Titus and make sure he stays down, Sam."

"No," Sam said. "I want you to do that. You're quicker than I am, and I want Titus out of the line of fire as fast as we can manage it."

Tucker didn't argue. He just nodded.

They hurried back to the spot where they had left the other three men. Duane, Gabby, and Randy lowered their guns as Sam and Tucker came into view.

"Did you find 'em?" Gabby asked.

Sam nodded, and in as few words as possible sketched in the situation. "I'm asking the three of you to run a big risk," he concluded. "When you charge the place, you'll be outnumbered, and you can't just go in with all guns blazing because you might hit Titus. You'll have to pick your shots mighty carefully until Tucker and I come down that bluff."

"But you'll take them by surprise and turn the tide in our favor," Duane said. "It's a fine plan, Sam. Let's do it."

"I'm ready," Gabby said with a nod.

Sam looked at Randy. The young man hadn't really been tested in battle, and although he looked nervous, his voice was strong as he said, "You've gone out on a limb for me more'n once, Mr. Blaylock. I'm ready, too. I won't let you down."

Sam clapped a hand on his shoulder. "I know you won't, Randy," he said. "And from here on out, it's Sam, all right."

A grin stretched across Randy's face as he said, "Sure, Sam."

In a matter of moments, they made their final plans, and Sam and Tucker slipped off through the woods again. This time they circled wide around the outlaw camp so they could reach the top of the bluff without being seen. It was about thirty feet high and too steep for horses, but a man could climb it.

Tucker led the way and Sam followed, trusting the younger man's instincts and sense of direction. He couldn't hear the voices or smell the smoke from the camp. But after a few minutes the bluff loomed up in front of them. Tucker swarmed up it like a monkey. Sam took a little longer and had to grab hold of a few roots that stuck out of the bluff to steady himself as he climbed. He was slightly winded when he reached the top, but he would have to catch his breath while they were moving. There was no time to rest.

He still hadn't heard any screaming, but that couldn't last.

He smelled smoke again and knew they were close. Tucker went to hands and knees and so did Sam, pushing his Henry rifle along the ground beside him. A few more yards and Tucker dropped to his belly. Sam crawled up alongside him.

They were at the edge of the bluff, looking down at the lean-tos and the rest of the camp. Tucker had led them unerringly to where they needed to be. Sam saw Ramsey standing in front of the lean-to where Pike was. From here he got his first good look at the outlaw leader's Satanic face. Ramsey looked like he might be as bad as Pike made him out to be.

A few feet away, the ape-like Holcomb still had hold of Titus, who was pale with terror as Holcomb held a Bowie knife to the side of his face.

" . . . the truth, Pike, we'll make it fast for you,"

Ramsey was saying. "I'll send a couple of the boys to retrieve that loot right now. But if you've lied to me and they come back without it, you'll be mighty sorry."

"I didn't lie," Pike's voice came from inside the lean-to. "You can let the boy go now."

Ramsey smiled and said, "I don't think so. I think I'll let Holcomb cut him a little, just to make sure you're not trying to pull a fast one."

"It's the truth, I tell you!" Pike said. "Don't – "

Sam had already drawn a bead on Holcomb with the Henry. Firing from up here now meant giving up the element of surprise, but it couldn't be helped. Sam wasn't going to let his son be mutilated.

But as Ramsey turned his head to nod a command to Holcomb, Duane Beatty burst out of the brush, yelling something in French he must have learned from his Cajun grandmother and firing the ivory-handled revolver in his fist. One of the guards doubled over as Duane's slug punched into his guts.

Holcomb pulled back a little from Titus in surprise, and Sam caressed the Henry's trigger. The whipcrack of the shot added to the sudden confusion in the camp. Holcomb's head jerked as the .44-40 round bored through his brain and exploded out the other side in a pink spray of blood and bone. He let go of Titus and dropped, limp as a rag doll.

Tucker had already slid halfway down the slope, moving so fast the eye could hardly follow him. He launched himself in a headlong dive that sent him crashing into Titus. The impact swept the boy off his feet.

Sam swung the rifle toward Ramsey as he worked the lever, but before he could fire, Orion Pike exploded out of the lean-to and tackled Ramsey. Sam caught a glimpse of bright red blood on the old man's shirt, then the two struggling figures rolled back into the crude structure, out of sight.

Gabby's shotgun boomed and Randy's rifle cracked as they pitched into the fight as well. Shots blasted from the outlaws as they clawed out their holstered guns. Sam went down the slope in a hurry, half-bounding and half-falling. He lost his balance part of the way down and slid to the bottom. When he surged to his feet he had the Henry braced against his hip. He cranked off four more shots as fast as he could work the rifle's lever and saw one of the outlaws go down in a limp sprawl.

Randy collapsed as one of his legs was knocked out from under him by owlhoot lead. He dropped his rifle but managed to grab and lift the weapon in time to shoot the man drawing a bead on him.

One of the outlaws made a break for the horses, but Gabby's shotgun boomed again. The double charge of buckshot shredded the man and tossed him to the ground in a bloody heap.

A few yards from Sam, Tucker hovered above Titus, still shielding the boy's body with his own, but the Tranters were in Tucker's hands now, spewing flame and death in a rolling roar of gun-thunder. A thick cloud of powdersmoke hung over the camp.

Only a couple of the outlaws were still on their feet, and they must have seen that the fight was hopeless because they threw their guns down and thrust their hands in the air. Confident that his friends had the situation in hand, Sam swung toward the lean-to where Pike and Ramsey had been struggling. Pike had Ramsey down just inside the lean-to. The old man's hands were locked around Ramsey's throat under that spade beard. The outlaw leader's face was blue and his tongue stuck out. He was as dead as he would ever be, but Pike was still choking him.

"Threaten . . . that boy . . . will you?" Pike panted as he squeezed. "You son of a – "

Sam wrapped an arm around Pike and pulled him away. "Orion!" he said. "Orion, he's dead! It's over!"

Pike turned his head to look at Sam with an uncomprehending gaze. Slowly, he seemed to realize what Sam had said. Then Pike asked in a croaking voice, "The boy?"

Sam glanced around and saw that Tucker was helping Titus to his feet. Titus didn't appear to be hurt.

"He's all right."

Pike smiled. "Good," he said.

Then his eyes rolled back in their sockets and he went limp in Sam's arms.

21

Several minutes passed before Pike's eyelids fluttered open again. By that time, Gabby was wrapping bandages torn from a dead man's shirt around the deep bullet gouge in Randy's thigh and Duane had finished tying up the two outlaws they had taken prisoner. Tucker had checked to make sure all the others were dead.

Pike was laid out on a bedroll with Sam on one side of him and Titus on the other. Sam had already moved the blood-soaked shirt aside enough to know that the old man had been shot through and through several times when Ramsey and the rest of the outlaws jumped him and Titus. It was a wonder Pike had lived this long, as shot up as he was. He wouldn't last much longer.

Pike's eyes focused on Sam's face. "Sam," he whispered. "The boy . . ."

"I'm right here, Mr. Pike," Titus said. "I'm sorry you got hurt. I'm so sorry."

Pike shook his head a little. "Not your fault . . . son. Always knew . . . this day was comin' . . . sooner or later. Can't live like I have . . . without comin' to a bad end. I had me some . . . high times along the way, though." Pike looked at Sam again. "You know what . . . this boy o' yours done, Sam? He came after me . . . brought me some food and money . . . said it might help me . . . get away from Ramsey. Said he'd ride with me a ways . . . keep me comp'ny . . . Didn't know we were gonna . . . ride right into Ramsey and his bunch."

Titus looked across Pike's body and asked miserably, "Pa, should he be talkin' so much? Shouldn't he rest?"

"Let the man speak his piece, son," Sam said.

Pike chuckled. "You always was smart, Sam . . . just like I said. You always knew . . . what's what. But here's somethin' . . . you didn't know. I lied to you about what I done . . . when I run out on Ramsey. I took pert near . . . twenty thousand dollars with me . . . more'n half the loot he had cached. Hid it in a place 'bout ten miles north o' here . . . Look for a hill . . . with one lightnin' blasted tree on top of it . . . You'll find a little cave . . . at the bottom o' that hill. The money's in there . . . You know . . . what to do with it."

"Sure, Orion," Sam said. "I'll take care of it."

A soft sigh came from the dying old man. "Good. Knew I could . . . count on you . . . We always had . . . good times . . . didn't we?"

"Good times. I'll never forget 'em."

"Yeah. Tell your boy . . . he's a mighty fine . . ."

Titus leaned closer. "I'm right here, Mr. Pike. You can tell me. I'm right here."

Quietly, Sam said, "He can't tell you anything, son." He reached out and gently closed the sightless, staring eyes.

Titus sniffled and forced down a sob. "He wasn't a bad man," he choked out. "Not really."

"Not as bad as some," Sam agreed. "Better than a lot." He stood up and held out a hand. "Come on, Titus. Folks are waiting at home for you. For all of us."

#

Mitchell McCarthy hurried away from the ferry landing toward his newspaper office as Sam, Tucker, and Duane rode off Eustace Kendall's ferry the next day, leading the horses ridden by the two outlaws. The sullen prisoners' hands were tied behind their backs again. McCarthy probably wanted to get out an extra issue of the paper.

The commotion caused by their arrival in Shooter's Cross reached the marshal's office ahead of them. Everett Tolliver was waiting for them in front of the building. The federal lawman, Josiah Herrick, was with him.

"Those are two of Ramsey's men!" Herrick exclaimed.

"That's right, Marshal," Sam said. "One of my men is bringing in a wagon with the bodies of Ramsey, Orion Pike, and the rest of the gang. He'll be here in a little while. In the meantime . . ." Sam untied the canvas bag he had lashed to his saddle. He threw it on the ground at Herrick's feet. "There's a little less than twenty thousand dollars of loot in there, Marshal. I don't know where the rest of what they stole is hidden, but maybe you can get these two to tell you." He leaned forward in the saddle and added in a voice as hard as flint, "I don't much give a damn either way."

"What happened, Sam?" Tolliver asked as he looked up at the riders. "I have to admit, after what happened yesterday, I had a few doubts about you . . ."

"Gabby will tell you the whole story when he gets here with the wagon." Sam glanced toward the newspaper office. "And McCarthy will blow it all out of proportion and find some way to make everything my fault. But you'll know the truth, anyway."

"There are still some folks around here who don't agree with everything McCarthy says in that paper of his, Sam."

Sam shrugged and lifted his reins. "Right now I don't give much of a damn about that, either."

"Wait just a minute," Herrick blustered as Sam started to turn his horse away and Duane and Tucker handed the reins of the outlaws' mounts to Everett Tolliver. "You still interfered with a federal lawman in the course of his duties! I don't care what else you did, you can still be charged for that, Blaylock!"

Without looking around, Sam said, "You want me, you know where to find me."

The place that from now on was going to be his home, come hell or high water.

Rancho Diablo.

Made in the USA
Lexington, KY
26 June 2012